John Blake White

The Forgers

A dramatic poem

John Blake White

The Forgers
A dramatic poem

ISBN/EAN: 9783337335359

Printed in Europe, USA, Canada, Australia, Japan

Cover: Foto ©Andreas Hilbeck / pixelio.de

More available books at **www.hansebooks.com**

THE FORGERS;

A DRAMATIC POEM,

BY

JOHN BLAKE WHITE, Esqr.,

OF CHARLESTON, S. C.

AUTHOR OF

"Foscari; or, The Venetian Exile," "Mysteries of the Castle;
or, The Victim of Revenge," "Modern Honor"
and other Dramatic Poems.

Performed at the Charleston Theatre, 1825 and 1826.

Reprinted from Southern Literary Journal of
March, 1837, by order of his Son,

OCTAVIUS A. WHITE, M. D., LL. D.

OF NEW YORK.

1899.

THE FORGERS:

A DRAMATIC POEM,

By JOHN BLAKE WHITE, Esq.,

OF CHARLESTON, S. C.

REPRINTED FROM SOUTHERN LITERARY JOURNAL, MARCH, 1837,
BY ORDER OF HIS SON,

OCTAVIUS A. WHITE, M.D., LL.D.,

OF NEW YORK.

DRAMATIS PERSONÆ.

Mordaunt, *a wealthy and respectable merchant.*
Leonard Mordaunt, *his son.*
Charles Ridgeford, *a dissipated friend to Leonard Mordaunt.*
Horatio Wardlaw, *a pious friend of the same.*
Fenton, *a wealthy merchant, friend to Mordaunt, sen.*
Freeman, *a youth, clerk to Mordaunt, sen.*

Mrs. Mordaunt, *mother of Leonard Mordaunt.*
Laura, *daughter to Fenton.*
Harriet, *sister to Wardlaw.*
Celestina, *sister to Ridgeford.*

· Sprite, Masks, Officers, Master of Ceremonies, Pall Bearers, Servants, &c., &c.

ACT I.—SCENE I.

An apartment in the house of RIDGEFORD—CELESTINA, *alone, looking through a casement on the full moon which is just rising.*

Cel. Thou eloquent dumb witness of my shame,—
I loathe thy beams !—I stooped, curs'd thought ! to make
My conquest sure,—my failure, not my fault,
I mourn ! The heart that's wanton of its boon,

Unworthy proves to be retained in love,
And soon, as little worth, is flung away!
Ah! there I failed, and now remorse corrodes
My soul, changing its vital flood to gall!
'Twas on a night, resplendent as this is,
When at my feet, a paragon of worth,
He lay, my slave.—A cloud passed o'er the scene,
And pestilential grief now racks my brain!—
Mordaunt, Mordaunt! fain would I resign thee,
Could I the deep foundations of my love
Root up, and blot from memory the past,
Though false, memorials of thy plighted faith!
Detested thought! – Fond memory be still!
Rest, rest till vengeance hath appeased my hate!

Enter RIDGEFORD.

Ridg. Ha, Celestina—are you here alone?
What! Ruminating on the stars?—if so,
I pray you cast my horoscope, and tell
What future destiny they do portend.
Cel. My mind is wrapped too deep in inward thought,
To read the stars, or scan another's fate.
A soul perturbed looks not beyond itself.—
Have you of late seen Mordaunt in your walks?
Ridg. I have; we parted brief time since.
Cel. Indeed!
Ridg. You challenge as of right. One might infer,
To hear your speech, that he'd surrendered all,
And vowed obedience to you, as—your lord.
Cel. Come, come; I pray you, do not chafe me thus.
You find me in no fitting mood to jest!—
Time hurries on, and I must bluntly speak
The wrongs 'twere idle longer to disguise.
Ridg. Well, speak; I'm neither dull to hear, nor slow
To execute your will. Proceed!
Cel. Attend.
You know I loved him —Mordaunt, yea, I loved
With more than woman's ardor: I adored
The earth whereon he trod. But, once deceived,
And who can e'er forgive! If brother's heart
Beats in your breast, you will avenge my wrongs,
Though you've long stood a driveller by my side!
Ridg. You speak at random, like a fool!
Cel. Well, well!
Yet nerve enough I have to follow him,
Which I will surely do, have I but life,
With fierce, unceasing vengeance to the grave,

Unless atonement in the dust be made.

Ridg. Be calm! why rave on thus?—You seem to me
A maniac turned! Sure I've already done,
Yea, still am doing in your cause, far more
Then hell-born malice need devise.

Cel.   Pray, what?

Ridg. Who leads him to the gambling-house by night?
Who undermines his character by day?
Who dissipates his time? Who wastes his health?
Who tempts him, day by day, to drain the cup,
And add intemperance to his other crimes?
Think you, that, but for me, Mordaunt would prove
Bankrupt in purse and reputation, thus?—
Yet all for sake of you, unthankful girl!

Cel. More, then, you merit than you'd credit for:
Accept a sister's gratitude.—Well, then,
Forgive my haste; 'twas passion moved me thus.
When urged by that, I know not what I do,
Or think, or speak. But come, I'm calm—proceed.

Ridg. Mordaunt, if managed with discretion true,
The hand of Laura Fenton never gains.
Whether you'll deem him worthy of your hand,
Defeated thus, you shall yourself decide;
Though I will lay him at your feet, rest sure!

Cel. Think not I'd take this remnant of a man,
For he'll be naught else when I've sped my shaft,
And place him o'er my destiny, supreme!

Ridg. Sister of mine, I would so judge your mind.

Cel. Why should I dwell on my own wrongs alone!
'True, they are worthy of your deep revenge,
For deeper stain ne'er blurred a sister's fame!
Still would I have you not forget your own.
Remember, Laura, but for him, was yours,
And might be still, if close you press your suit.
She's wealth, with all things worthy of your grasp.
So deep the hazard play in such a game!
I rest upon you, with a sister's love,
Well counting on your wisdom and your nerve!

Ridg. 'Tis but of late the worst has reached my ear,
Finding that Laura pays his suit regard.
Had I not hoped he would have claimed your hand
Full long ere this, he should have made amends
For pangs he caused your doating heart to feel.
But brotherly regard restrained my arm;
So traced me out a slow though certain course,
Which makes our triumph glorious in the end!

Cel. Pray you go on, I like to hear your views.

Ridg. By any plot devised, we should defeat
This purposed marriage.—Time is all we need :
Time, that most sure and deadly foe to fame.
    Cel. That Laura loves him, cannot be denied.
    Ridg. Her native prudence will withhold her vows,
Could she but meet him as he's oft of late,
The victim of intemperance and debauch.
    Cel. E'en Fenton too——
    Ridg.   His prudence is well known,—
He will reject his claims beyond all doubt,
So soon as we disclose his character.—
Postpone their union, and they never wed :
Expose his foibles and he turns to you,—
Reject him, if you please—he's lost :
Accept—your clouds in azure melt away.
But once exhibit him to Laura's eyes,
The gaping object of a world's just scorn ;
Steep him in Wine, then thrust him in her path,
To gibe and gibber like some mountain ape,
My word upon it, she abandons him ;
Yea, were the altar decked to plight their troth.
    Cel. You are indeed my oracle !
    Ridg.   Then mark !
The mask we've now on foot, will soon afford
Befitting field for active enterprise.
Mere novice must I be indeed, should I
Expedients lack, to make our project good.
To chance, we needs must leave minute detail,
Whilst subtilty directs our grander moves.
    Cel. But look ! here Wardlaw comes,
    Ridg. Let's change the theme.
    Cel. A Comet, to the sun, moves not with pace
More swift, than he to Laura's ear.
    Ridg. Freight this free shallop well with poisoned store,
And let it glide full laden into port.

Enter WARDLAW.

You're welcome—in right fitting time you come
To mingle sympathy with our regret—
Our thoughts were turned on Mordaunt's evil speed.
    Ward. No serious evil has befallen him ?
    Ridg. Merely the loss of some few thousand dimes,
Which, though at present, he can ill afford,
Fair Laura's coffers will make good, full soon.
    Ward. Tempests may sweep the merchant from the sea,
And scatter his rich produce on the waves ;
Yet he proves bankrupt ne'er who sternly keeps

Honor and piety to guide his course.
Shall I lament that some commercial ill
Lights on his house? for such your words import.
   Cel. 'Twere good, if nothing worse beset his weal,
For then his bark, secure might cleave the waves
Of this tempestuous life ;—but some make sport
Of honor as with dice,—are free with oaths,
Drink deep and gamble, proffer vows, betray,—
Yet, current pass, as honorable men.
Mordaunt perhaps, exception proves in these.
   Ridg. Why Mordaunt, true, drinks freely with his friends,
And sports as freely with his worldly trash,
Yet, he most justly boasts an honest name—
The debt of honor he has late incurred,—
Will soon be paid, forgotten be as soon.
'Tis not the first, nor will it be the last.
   Cel. If last, 'twere least—Intemperance, far worse,
Besets his daily and his nightly path.
No friend of Laura, more than I, laments
The mournful sacrifice she early makes.
   Ward. Yet, draw, I pray, the veil of charity,
O'er deeds, that sterner justice may condemn :
Thus may we pardon hope for, when we err.
   Cel. 'Tis strange, that, you, the advocate become
Of crimes, 'gainst which the righteous cry aloud ;
Yet Laura's ills will not the lighter prove,
When she, cold charity, from others seeks.
   Ward. I only would avert a shaft that's aimed
'Gainst absent reputation. Be the faults
Of Mordaunt what they may, let's strive to mend,
Not publish them.
   Cel. I deemed it merely just,
To you, as Laura's friend, thus free to speak,
Trusting you would right promptly shield her heart,
Glance the averted arrow, where it may.—
You join the maskers, I presume ?
   Ward.   Not I.
   Ridg. The Masquerade, that fête expected long,
Excludes at present, every other thought.
The curious world, on eager tiptoe stands,
Anxious to catch, e'en glimpse behind the scene ;
Such is man's love, to forerun things to come.
   Cel. I'll venture, you have played the spy.—
   Ridg.   One Swain
The blackguards acts in costume all complete.
Another takes the character of ape,
And apes the ape, to admiration.—Then,

Two will attempt to play off, puss and pug,
And fight and scratch and run about the halls;
Doing in all, as puss and pug are wont.
    Ward. What worthy pastime for immortal souls!
    Cel. A canting age is this in which we live!
Rejecting pleasures for the lack of taste,
Railing at joys it has not sense to feel!
It fills me ever with disgust!—Adieu!   [*Exit.*
    Ward. So now, good Ridgeford, I would say one word,
On subjects that concerns our Mordaunt's fate.
    Ridg. No one more ready ear than I,—
    Ward.   No doubt.
You've learnt, perhaps, that he affianced was
To Laura, fairest in our maiden train,—
    Ridg. And will be wedded soon, if fame speaks true,
Nor less good luck I wish him, in my soul!
    Ward. Much as my heart inclines me to his cause,
Still, I dare not in ready mood respond
To such ejaculation. Whilst his course,
Eccentric as it is, concerned himself
Alone, however painful to look on,
I dared not speak: It seemed like sowing seed
To grow on stony ground,—but now 'tis changed;
For soon, another's weal is linked with his;
So friendship bids no longer silence keep,—
And needs must warn him 'gainst the brink he treads.
    Ridg. What would you more, than have them marry
        forth?
A youth no sooner has resigned the world,
And taken to himself a prudent wife,
Then straight a man, he proves, reformed and true;
Who ever knew a rake reclaimed, 'till wed?
    Ward. I ne'er subscribe to like philosophy;—
Intemperance on intemperance daily feeds,
And he that feebly grasps the cup in youth,
In manhood or in age, a maniac dies.
    Ridg. The coward only fears the bowl!
    Ward.   Be wise!
Sport not, pray, Ridgeford, with a cause so grave!
I treat in serious mood, and crave your aid,
So trust you will not tamper in this mood.
    Ridg. Well, speak.—What would you have me do?
    Ward.   The world
Well knows the sway you hold o'er Mordaunt's mind,
To good or ill account the same. To you,
I make appeal in this grave enterprise,
Not doubting to obtain your friendly aid.

Ridg. Better seek aid at more experienced hands.
Poor pilot, one, whose barque's already wrecked.
    Ward. What honors Rome decreed who rescued life!
Yet how far greater glory, his, who saves
A soul alive, and rescues it from hell.
    Ridg. Hold not, kind Wardlaw, in such fulsome strain,
It suits me not,—In my own way I act.—
I never was, nor will be led by man.
Intemperance, that hard besetting vice,
Philosophy and firmness may subdue,
And when that happy conquest is obtained,
You may command me, as you deem it meet.
    Ward. If only on Philosophy we rest,
Our hopes are vain,—some arm more potent still
Must guide our course, else all our labor's lost.
    Ridg. We'll meet again, and graver conference hold.
    Ward. 'Tis needless more to meet.—Good night.
    Ridg.   Good night.
I go in haste to join our friend: Adieu!   [*Exeunt.*

SCENE II.

An elegant Drawing room, in the house of Mordaunt, Senr.

MR. AND MRS. MORDAUNT.

    Mr. M. The wealth of Rothschild even, can't supply
The spendthrift cravings of a son like ours.
Peruvian mines could not make good such wants.
    Mrs. M. Why speak of mines, and cast them in the scale,
With one, whom I have treasured in my soul,
Yea, garnered up, within my heart of hearts?
    Mr. M. Who pray, more liberal has been than I?
Domestics, carriages of every sort,
Racers, and hounds, yea, every thing, indeed,
That could divert the mind or please the taste,
Have long his utmost wants forerun, yet, still
What is his gratitude for all these gifts!
Intemperance! I blush to name the vice!
Demands, and bills, and drafts extravagant,
Pour in upon me daily.
    Mrs. M.   Hapless youth!
    Mr. M. A draft, in favor of some unknown hand,
Was late presented for a heavy sum;
But this our house, in honest part, refused.
    Mrs. M. Disgrace, far worse than death! What value's
        wealth,
If not to gratify those hearts we love?

I'd barter all we own, nay, crawl the earth,
Rather than heap such shame upon our son!
Ah! rather were I in my silent grave,
Where I must shortly be, dishonored thus!
    Mr. M. A parent, am I not in duty bound
To know the end of prodigal demands,
Before I give my purse to sanction them?
    Mrs. M. A noble soul like his, disdains to give,—
I prize him higher for his manly pride,—
A slave's base reck'ning for each cent he spends:
I'd have him starve, ere thus to condescend!
You're undeserving, Mordaunt, of a son
Like ours.—Still, all, I trust, will soon be well.
Dear Laura Fenton will requite his worth,
And make him independent of a world!
All that I blush for, is, that he must go
A beggar, almost, to her father's house!
    Mr. M. Such shafts fly back on those who launch them
        forth.
How long ere this, might Laura have been his,
Had fell Intemperance not dashed the cup,
That Virtue had presented to his lip!
    Mrs. M. Thus are his youthful foibles treasured up,
To be forever cast into his face;—
Is this the part a tender parent acts?
    Mr. M. Why thus afflict my heart?
    Mrs. M.   'Twill sure break mine!
Reflect you, Mordaunt, on our Leonard's fate!
Think of the wound his honor has sustained,—
And for no better cause than senseless trash!
Stung to the quick at sense of wounded pride,
He shrinks with horror from the vulgar gaze,
And flies for refuge to oblivious draughts,
While narrow parents count their gilded dross!
    Mr. M. Such keen, such harsh reproach I merit not:
Nor can I longer bear it! Heaven forfend,
That, wild extravagance and guilty joys,
May not the ruin and destruction prove
Of him, and of his doating parents too!   [*Exit.*
    Mrs. M. To think that he, who is my soul's first pride,
And whom I've nurtured with maternal care,
Jealous to have him tread in honor's path,
Should at this day, a humble suppliant stoop,
For dross, to which I scorn to give a name!
This world, indeed, is cursed enough with ills;
Why strew them in the path of those we love?
But here the dear one comes!

Enter MORDAUNT.

Ah, why so pale?
Speak, beloved Leonard,—tell your mother all.
Mor. O would, kind madam, I were left alone!
Mrs. M. Your air distracts me, Leonard. Here, repose!
Pray let me bathe your temples. You seem faint!
Mor. Good mother, give me rest. My head! my head!
Mrs. M. Ah! 'tis the heart, not head, too well I know,
That is affected most!
Mor.   Leave me my heart:
'Tis all I have to boast of as my own,—
Some drink!—some drink!
Mrs. M.   What will you chose, my love?
                              [*Rings a bell.*
Mor. Prithee, kind mother, anything. My tongue
Is dried to parchment,—and a little Wine
Is sure specific 'gainst headache, or grief.
                              [*Enter a Servant.*
Mrs. M. Bring forth the salver.   [*Exit Servant.*
You're too much fatigued:
Some slight refreshment may not prove amiss.
Mor. Press not your hand too heavy on my head.
Good mother, you but suffocate me thus.
Pray let me breathe awhile!

[*Re-enter servant, bearing in an elegant silver waiter, with
    decanters of various sorts of Wine, Brandy, &c., &c.*]
                    Serve out a glass.
[*She fills a glass and Mordaunt drinks repeatedly.*]
So now, set by the stand. [*Exit Servant, with waiter, &c.*
Mrs. M.   How now?
Mor.   Revived
A little,—Speak not loud,—my temples throb.
Mrs. M. I well devise the cause of your concern,
                    (*leaning over him tenderly.*)
And shall right measures take, to give you ease.
Your father's to be ruled with skilful hands;
So rest your cares upon a mother's love.
Mor. I boast no father, no, nor mother now!
The world and all its joys are naught to me,
Since parents' hearts are turned to steel!
Mrs. M.   Not so!
Have I not proved a mother, bland and kind?—
My Leonard can't of aught accuse me, sure!
Had I the world, I'd cast it at his feet;
Yea, give the stars, as play things for his sport,
Could I but see those cheeks lit up with smiles,

And find youth's blithesome days return, once more!

Mor. Be still!—My father comes!—I must be dumb.

Enter MR. MORDAUNT.

Mr. M. E're I accept the draft you lately drew,
I think young man, I may demand to learn,
If not on what account, for whom, at least,
It is designed.

Mor.   You have become indeed
Fastidious, Sir,—Till late, you ne'er refused
My draft, however drawn.

Mr. M.   And therefore, Sir,
Advantage taking of my love, you prove
Unworthy of my tender trust!

Mrs. M.   Such words
Are sure enough to drive him to despair!

Mr. M. My son, towards whom I looked, thro' hope's
          bright maze,
To crown his father's age with joy, brings naught,
Alas! but sorrow to his parent's heart!
Stooping from rank, where friends and fortune are,
The dissolute and vile, are your compeers.
The tavern, and the brothel, and the broil,
Are the resources of my only child!

Mor. Rail on! rail on!—I must endure it all!

Mrs. M. This is enough to sink me to the grave!

Mr. M. Enough to drive a father mad! Yet, still,
Still must I bear it, for 'tis now too late!

Mor. And though all base, and infamous I prove,
I scorn a niggard, tho' a father's hand!

Mr. M. Ingrate!—But no!—a father's bitter curse,
Shall not fall on that head!—Let me begone!
Before some word escape my hasty lips,
That may forever poison all your hopes!—
No more you merit favors at my hands.
So henceforth learn, my purse, nay, e'en my heart,
Is closed against you, ever!   [*Exit.*

Mor.   This is good!
Now, this is treatment for an only child,
Who must be clad in Summer's smiles, so soft,
While Winter's tempests freeze his soul!

Mrs. M.   My child,
Be calm, be calm,—all shall be well.

Mor.   'Tis well!
Let it rage on!—I am accustomed thus.

Mrs. M. Come to my closet, 'till the storm is past.
What would I not, to give that bosom rest!—
Command me as you will,—come follow me. [*Exeunt.*

ACT II.—SCENE I.

An elegant chamber in the house of MORDAUNT, SEN.—
MORDAUNT *lies stretched upon a rich couch, having just
awoke from disordered sleep.—Decanters, wine glasses,
pens, ink, &c., on the table.*

Mor. Conduct him in. (*Addressing a servant who is re-
tiring.*)
Good morning to my friend!

Enter RIDGEFORD.

Ridg. Long since has morning cast her night-cap off,
Bowing her grey head to the working world.
'Tis pressing hard mid-day; as well, good night,
As pipe good morn at noon.
Mor.   Noon then it is.
I have a raging head-ache.
Ridg.   So have I.
But who fares well, after such night's carousal?
How stand accounts with you?
Mor.   My usual luck:
Most frightfully against me!—all was loss.
Since rude dame Fortune turns her back on me,
'Tis time I change this gambling course of mine.
Ridg. Then, bury deep in some sequestered cave:
As well be dead, as not in fashion's round.
Why, gambling is the soul of trade, these days.
Without it, what is life? A desert waste.
The world itself's but one wide gambling board,
Where men,—and women too,—in whispers speak,
When ill of them,—are very gamblers, all.
There, men in speculation deep, entrust
To chance the penny, to make sure the pound:
Venturing most freely, when at other's risk.
The lawyer, doctor, merchant, statesman, judge,
All gamblers turn. Let them but win the stake,
What ill may fall on others, none regards.
If they but fortune win, they win the world,
And certain are of honor, friends, and fame.
Mor. I know not, Ridgeford, how I reached my couch
So steeped I was in wine's subduing waves.
Some guardian hand supported me.
Ridg.   'Twas mine.
Who e'er deserts a friend in time of need?
Mor. My funds were never at so low an ebb.
My prudent father has locked up his stores,
And even turned me, stranger from his heart.

So thus, behold me, thrown upon my wits.

Ridg. 'Tis well when fate decrees no harder lot.
That it would come to this, I long foresaw :
But them, as kin, I only count, who're kind.
'Tis high time, sure, you drop your leading strings.

Mor. 'Tis time I burst them, you should rather say
Each day they do become more galling bonds!

Ridg. I love you all the better for that speech :
It augurs well, and proves you are a man.
Have you, of late, bethought you of the scheme
Upon the subject of the loan ?

Mor. I have,
But like it not, I must in candor state.

Ridg. Point out some wise objection : None I see.
A few brief weeks, you say, makes Laura yours,
With all the splendid fortunes of her house.
Now, where's the crime to forestal use of that,
Which must eventually be at our will,
To be disposed of, as we fitting think ?

Mor. Consistent with philosophy, I own ;
Nor does this view of it excite my cares ;
Still, Ridgeford,——

Ridg. Scruples. I presume, at law !
How oft, from such false fears, in timid souls,
Important ends are lost ! The man of nerve,
Unlocks him treasures, and he rolls in wealth !
When yours,—and soon, full soon, it will be yours,—
Who then dare call you to your strict account ?

Mor. I have bestowed much serious thought on all
You've urged, and feel inclined to try the move ;
Though I confess, I have some secret qualms.

Ridg. The weak misgivings of our grand-dames' days !
I understand you,—moral twitches ? Ha !—
On this head learn, then, I've no more to urge ;
I thought I had exhausted all long since :
You are unfit to manage great designs.
Give up the scheme, let's think of it no more,—
A beggar live, a beggar learn to die !

Mor. Yet why, kind Ridgeford, why thus hasty grown ?
First, cast an eye on this. [*handing him a paper.*] A rude
    attempt,
A mere essay, to test my steady hand.

Ridg. Upon my honor, excellent, indeed !
Fac-simile to all intents, I vow !
I never thought your hand or pen so firm.

Mor. Compare it first with these originals.
    [*Producing other signatures, which they carefully
    compare.*]

I've not been idle since we broached the scheme.

Ridg. Sly rogue you are! Who dreampt of this?

Mor. Think you
'T will bear close scrutiny?—Compare,—compare.

Ridg. No doubt of it; 't will stand the nicest test.
You are a prodigy of graphic taste!
'Tis wondrous close!—Fenton himself, although
He scan it with a lynx's eyes, dare not
Dispute the signature.

Mor. Still I protest——

Ridg. You grow more timid than the mountain fawn!
You'll be afraid to walk in sunshine soon,
Lest your own shadow fright you, 'gainst the wall.

Mor. But, did we venture, what sum should we draw?

Ridg. Draw boldly for a liberal one.

Mor. For five?—

Ridg. Ten thousand rather say—a hundred e'en:
A sum, thus large, the seldomer you draw,
And less the risk.

Mor. That's true! Well, fill the blank.

Ridg. Why boldly, man, fill up the blank yourself.
I hate these squeamish fits!—They ill become
A man, and badly suit some whimpering girl.
Here, take the pen and make your work complete!

[Handing a pen to MORDAUNT.
The pen 's a talisman, a magic wand,
That blasts, or crowns the lover's ardent hopes.
It is the harbinger of peace and war.
It dooms the culprit, and sets free the slave.
It scatters to the winds the miser's hoards,
Dispensing joy, through liberal souls, like ours.
More trophies has it won, than e'er the sword,
And—Hold! Stay, stay your hand! Why tremble thus?
You'll ruin now, what you'd so well commenced.
Why tremble?

Mor. Ridgeford, I cannot go on!

Ridg. Because a novice only are you.—Pshaw!
'Twill end in naught unless I ply him well. [*Aside.*
Practice, good man, yes, practice makes us bold.
Come, come,—a glass or two. A few good draughts
Will give what most you need. [*They pour out wine.*

Mor. With all my heart!
My nerves are weak,—I've not yet tasted wine.
Fill up. A flowing bumper let us quaff,
To pliant maids and golden mines!

Ridg. Well said!
Mark!—Your hand now, trembles no more. It seems

As firm, yea, even as a rock.

Mor. The pen!
Give me the pen.—I will no longer haggle. [*Writes.*
There—I have filled the blanks—'tis now complete.

Ridg. You ne'er discovered truer nerve than now.

Mor. Still,—should this fail——

[*Handing the check over to* RIDGEFORD.

Ridg. Impossible! Fear not.
I'll stand between you and all worldly risk.
I warrant you it brings the needful pelf. [*Rings a bell.*

Mor. 'Tis done!

Ridg. Far rather say, 'tis well begun.
It smacks of ill, to augur ill so soon.

Enter SERVANT.

Mor. Send quickly our clerk, young Freeman, here.
[*Exit* SERVANT.
Have fallen in of late, with Wardlaw?

Ridg. Yes.
And oft'ner far, than well accords with taste.

Mor. He finds no longer interest in our sports,
But turns a pious heel on ancient friends.
Who would believe that he moved foremost, once,
In all the dissipated rounds of life?
Men look on now, with wonder at the change,
And ask, with gaping mouth, how such things come!

Ridg. Fools may!—For me, I hate your hypocrites.
Your health! [*Drinks.*

Mor. Good luck to this our enterprise!

Ridg. Amen!—A warm response to bold resolves.
[*They drink repeatedly.*

Enter FREEMAN.

Mor. Freeman, good day!—Please take this check to
bank
And cash it for me.

Free. Sir, I will.

Mor. Return
With all convenient speed. I need the draft.
Will take a glass?

Free. I pray, excuse me, sir.
[FREEMAN *bows and exit.*

Mor. Give us more wine. I tremble like a leaf!
This day, our destiny is sealed!—More wine!
'Tis, after all, one's safe resort, in need.
[*They drink several glasses.*

Ridg. When failed the bottle to bring man relief?
Wine bids us spurn these tenements of clay,
Exalting us companions for the gods!
The bottle, Mordaunt, 's man's best friend, at last:
It e'en sustains him in the hour of death,
Making his passport certain to that world,
Of which our sagest men so little know.
    Mor. Truly, this earth's mere pasture for the brute,
Where he must eat, and sleep, and drink, and die.
On ether mounted, we transcend the stars,
Where light, and scenes most bright, and sounds most soft,
And joy, and pure celestial harmony,
And bliss, and laughing mirth, and ardent hope,
All crowd the soul, and give foretaste of heaven!—
I feel, kind Ridgeford, you're my friend indeed!
    Ridg. And will be ever, till we part in death! [*Going.*
    Mor. My friend, my oracle!
    Ridg.   Repose a while.
    Mor. Desert me not!
    Ridg.   I will return anon.—
Seldom do men desert their monied friends.
                          [*Aside, and exit.*
    Mor. How oft, cursed wine, have I abjured thy rule,
Vowing, thy dread allurements to resist;
But, 'tis impossible!—What shall I do?
Is there no power on earth to save me!—No!
I've heard that wretches, in despair, have prayed;
And heaven has heard them, they do say; but I,
I know not why, I've thrown me on the earth,
And though I've poured my heart like water forth,
And mourned my sad condition like a child,
No language flows from these polluted lips
That I dare hope can reach the throne of Heaven;
For soon relief I find in that, alone,
From which my prayer had been to be preserved.
   [*Throws himself with great emotion on his couch, and
     falls asleep.*]

    Enter MRS. MORDAUNT, *treading lightly.*

    Mrs. M. He sleeps! How pale! how pale!—Here's too
    much light!   [*Drawing a curtain.*
I'd not disturb such slumber, soft, for worlds.
    Mor. O!
    Mrs. M. Leonard! speak!—What is the matter? Speak!
    Mor. Nothing! Ah, nothing!—What! are you so near?
    Mrs. M. Yes, and with mother's hand, I come to
    soothe!—

How, dearest Leonard! How fare you to-day?
Mor. Better, good mother, than of late; though, still
My brain is racked——
Mrs. M.   Why called you not on me?
These hands were wont to soothe, when pain beset
My child, in days gone by!
Mor.   You'll drive me mad!
O spare me, pray! I can't endure reproach!
Mrs. M. I come not, sure, to chide you! No,——ah, no!
But come, bright harbinger of comfort, come,
Even as angel, to bring sure relief.
 Mor. More soft than angel's, 'tis my mother's voice!
 Mrs. M. Such kind expressions, balm unto my soul!
Would, my dear Leonard, it were ever thus!——
Look up! Look up! [MORDAUNT *rises a little.*
      Your father's rage is past,——
A genial sun, after a summer's storm:
We know his weakness, and it grieves me sore,
To witness such harsh treatment at his hands.
But thus, he makes atonement for his fault.
Come, come, my child,——o'erlook all hasty speech:
Accept this paltry boon; unequal far,
      [*presenting a pocket-book.*
To such a mother's willing heart would give.
 Mor. Kind mother! let me kiss those hands!
  [*Starting up in great emotion, kisses her.*
Mrs. M.   My lips!
Kisses like these, repay me all you owe!
Your love, is all that I require. [*Embracing him tenderly.*
    Adieu!
You'll join us soon, I trust, with smiling eyes:
So heaven, its balmy dews shed on that brow! [*Exit.*

[MORDAUNT *hastily opens the pocket-book with much emo-*
  tion, and discovers several bank bills.]

 Mor. Eternal mercy! save a wretch condemned!
O, had this come some moments sooner! Then
Might I have been preserved! Freeman returns!
My adverse fate!

    Enter FREEMAN.

    Freeman!
Free.   The money, sir——
Mor. 'Tis paid, say you! No questions asked! As
 how?
Or when? or where? O, answer me!
 Free.   Sure not:

The house of Fenton stands too high——
Mor.   No doubt!
Enough! I thank you, Freeman! Leave me! Go!
Free. Before I go, will you not count the bills?
                    [*Laying the money on the table.*
Mor. Did you?
Free.   I did, at bank.
Mor.   'Tis well! 'Tis well!
You may retire, good Freeman,--'tis enough.
                [FREEMAN *bows respectfully, and exit.*
Poor boy! Thou 'rt scrupulous, because thou 'rt true!
Fain, fain I'd change conditions with thee!—ay,
The world to boot!—Could I undo this deed,
I'd gladly every hope on earth forego,
And give my life, poor ransom, for my fame!
My father! O my father! What will not
This cost thy heart!—Unworthy I, thy love!
                    [*Casts himself on his couch.*

Enter RIDGEFORD.

Ridg. The toils have taken I perceive! That's well.
                            [*Aside.*
What, man! amid such treasures, plunged in grief?
But late, you were in grief for lack of such;
Far fitter cause, forsooth.
Mor.   O Ridgeford! Ridgeford!
Ridg. Come, come; shake off this hypocondriac fit,
Becoming more the soul of Laura, far.
Mor. I'm sick!
Ridg.   Not yet of love.—A honey-moon
Would scarce suffice to sicken one of that;
So hold me on such topic two months hence,
When Laura's brightest charms are on the wane.
Mor. Withhold! withhold! I am not in right mood,
To touch at present on that subject!—Speak
Of vile debauches, drunken routs, mad broils,--
Themes more becoming me, than Laura's name!
Ridg. A sentimental paroxysm! Well!
Let work!--Himself will Richard be again,
Ere nightfall.
Mor.   Ridgeford! would that I were dead!
Ridg. Nay, Mordaunt! Would that thou wert wed!—
        The hyp!
The hyp! The green disease of girlhood, sure!
You have the money,—what more would you have?
" Put money," I, with sage Iago, say,
" Into thy purse."—Come, come; enough of this!

Let's be abroad. This chamber is a den.
You need fresh air.—Come, put your money up.
  Mor. Not I !--I cannot, will not touch it !
  Ridg.   Well!
Since suddenly thus scrupulous you've grown,
I'll be your banker : draw on me at sight.
  [*Puts the money and pocket-book into his pocket.*
Here ennui sits, in majesty sublime,
And spreads her murky blanket o'er our heads :
Fit canopy for anchorite alone.
Arise ! let 's join our merry friends abroad.
They'll chase these idle phantasies away,
And make you, as you ought to be,—a man !
Move forth : time flies : the maskers meet. The pipe,
Soft flute and merry viol, will dispel
Your gloom, and drive your fears afar.   [*Exeunt.*

SCENE II.

A vestibule to a ball room.—Crowds of ladies, splendidly dressed and masked, cross the apartment attended by the Master of Ceremonies.—Enter LAURA, *with several ladies of her train.*

  Master. Move this way, this way, lady, to the hall.
Attendants on your right will lead the way.

  [LAURA *and her attendants cross the vestibule and exeunt. Enter* CELESTINA *and her party of attendants, who also cross the apartment.*]
Make way, make way there. Throw the portals wide.
Clear all the avenues. The press will soon
Be great.—Make way there, all ; make way.   [*Exeunt.*

SCENE III.

A splendid ball room, brilliantly illuminated. A vast number of persons, in mask and domino, moving in various directions, to music. Several ludicrous figures, Harlequins, &c., &c., dancing in groups.

  1*st Mask.* Right grotesque figures these ;—let us look on.
We'll find no doubt, good point mid such a throng.
  2*d Mask.* Let's witness the encounter of those wits.
They seem disposed to run a tilt of words :
'Tis pleasing sport to look on bloodless strife.

  [*They retire to the back of the scene. Enter a mask in character of Bacchus, a Thyrsus in his hand, crowned with vine and ivy leaves, accompanied by a train, singing, dancing, &c., to music.*

All sing. Fill the bowl, with bumper flowing,
  Twine the garland. press the grape,
  While life's genial sun is glowing,
  Few my soft allurements 'scape.

[*They take Bacchus in their arms and exeunt. While
this scene is going on, enter* RIDGEFORD *and a Female
Mask in the character of Diana.*

Mask. Well, well; I've tortured you full well.
        [*Removing her mask.*
Ridg.   Indeed!
Who could have thought to have encountered you!
 Mask. And why not I, as some less worthy dame?
 Ridg. What swain so poor in gallantry, who'd dare
To banish Dian from her silvan scenes?
But, pure republican invention this!
The mask it is that levels all degrees,
Bringing the statesman and the hind on par.
 Mask. Thanks to kind Comus, for the happy change,
Who wisely sang in Milton's merry age;
" 'Tis only daylight that makes sin."

    So let's away,—
    Though tell me, pray,
   Where's Mordaunt found?
Ridg.   By light of moon,
    'Neath yon saloon,
   In love's chains bound;
  Breathing in ear, like tender tale,
  As turtles sigh on amorous gale.
Mask.   " Trip then, away,"
    And make no stay,"
  But "meet me all by break of day." [*Exit.*

 Enter CELESTINA *in haste, greatly discomposed.*

Ridg. Dear Celestina! What's the matter?—Speak!
 Cel. The matter ask!—With rage pluck out these eyes;
Did I not need them for my deep revenge!
 Ridg. Why rudeness offer unoffending eyes?
 Cel. Would they were basilisk's, a glance should kill!—
But now I left them! There's no room for doubt!
In yon saloon I've o'erheard enough!—
By all the powers of darkness, I protest!
While head and hand,—But let it pass!—'Tis well!
 Ridg. Tell me, I pray, who has thus dared transgress?
 Cel. Enough! Enough! I'm mistress of his fate,
Nor ask I aid, save what this hand can seize!
Conduct me to our coach.   [*Exeunt.*

[*While this scene is going on, enter Harlequin and a Female Mask. They come forward from the back of the Scene.*

Harl.   Fair lady, pray,
                    One moment stay,
                    Slight mark of pity show.
                    I've lost my love,
                    That gentle dove,
                    My Columbine, so true!
Lady.   Is that, then, all you rue?
Harl.   My loss were gain,
                    And no more pain,
                    Poor Harlequin would know,
                    If Columbine, you go.
Lady.   Learn them from me,
                    No sword of tree,
                    Can win fair lady's heart.
Harl.   Yet I, this truth impart,--
                    That, few can do,
                    Such wonders true,
                    As I, with steel or gold.
Lady.   Then, Harlequin, pray hold!
                    For all I ask,
                    As lover's task,
                    Are constancy and wealth,——
Harl.   Which have, if e'en by stealth.
                    Come then with me, and we will go,
                    Where the damask roses blow.
                    Prove but my constant Columbine,
                    A thousand balmy wreaths I'll twine,
                    And plant them on that brow.
Lady.   Away! away!
                    I'm yours, while--wealth endures. [*Exeunt.*

SCENE IV.

A splendid saloon, with large folding glass doors, and windows at the back, opening into a portico. Several tables, on which lie, in disorder, cards, back-gammon, chess boards, &c., &c. Music is heard, at a distance, as from an adjoining ball room. MORDAUNT *and* LAURA *seated at chess.*

Mor. Fair Laura, I have long projected this,--
Your knight is mine, so to your rook give check.
   Lau. My gallant knight assaults your queen. Escape,
Impossible,--Your king stands then exposed.

Mor. I ought to have foreseen and waived that blow.
You press me sore!—Your rook!
Lau. Your queen is mine.

[*During the progress of the game, a Sprite of pale and
hideous aspect glides in from the portico, unobserved by
MORDAUNT and LAURA, and takes its station at the
window, behind the chair of LAURA, overlooking the
board.*]

Mor. You failed to dwell discreetly on that move.
Now, gentle Laura, you are mine!
Lau. If so
You please.
Mor. Since it please you, that I should please
Myself, then sure I please, and—take you,—check!
Sprite. Thy check is false! Look to it! Look!
It much concerns thee—lady—look! [*Vanishes.*
[MORDAUNT *starts from his chair with horror.*
Lau. How now! how now! You would not play me,
false!
What is the matter?—Speak!—I pray explain!
Mor. A deadly pang shoots through my heart!
Lau. You're ill!
[*Several Masks cross the stage looking at* MORDAUNT,
and exeunt.
Mor. Throw back the curtain. Give me air!—I faint!
Lau. Your illness shocks me. I must fly for aid! [*Exit.*
Mor. Though fiend or angel, I unravel this!
[*Rushes into the portico. Shortly after he returns, much
agitated.*
No trace! Most strange! No footstep to be seen!
And from the portico, there's no escape,
For being palpable to flesh and blood!

Enter RIDGEFORD, *hastily.*

Ridg. What moves my friend?
Mor. Head ache! Naught else! naught
else!
To that, I am a martyr——
Ridg. When naught worse,
'Tis well.
Mor. Among the diverse masks, I'd learn,
What rickety, disjointed elfe, is that,
Which moves to-night, among this giddy throng?
Nor gait nor voice it has of this our world;
But, chattering like some hungry ape, it shrieks
And screams my guilt to all this wandering house,

With most malignant and vindictive triumph!

Ridg. Right subject are you for some madhouse, sure!
I know full well, each character and mask,—
Nor goblin such as you describe is here.
You dream.

    Mor.   It 'scaped there, through the portico.

    Ridg. There's no communication with the ground,
And a leap thence, inevitable death.

    Mor. Our guilty secret stands divulged!—I'm lost!

    Ridg. You play the idiot-brat!—Compose your mind.
Look where the mask and merry throng advance.
You must put on the man. A part like this,
Must not be acted here. Men's curious eyes
Are on us, nor will malice fail, to fix
Malignant cause for this.—Be on your guard.

    Mor. You have betrayed me!

    Ridg.   Conscience has :—naught else!
Some silly equivoke has scared you. Shame!
How many eyes are turned upon us. Note!

    Mor. Grievous to be, of idle wits, the scorn!
Let us retire.

    Ridg.   By no means!—Front it out!
This will not do!—Unless we laugh it off,
We shall become sure subjects of contempt!   [*Exeunt.*

ACT III.—SCENE I.

A handsome, though plain apartment in the house of WARD-
LAW. HARRIET *and* LAURA, *seated.*

    Lau. Last night, as we were moving from the ball,
Into our coach, this scrip was rudely thrust
By hand unknown, that disappeared so soon.

    Har. 'Tis hardly legible, though plain to mark
Affected negligence in every line ;
Intended to misguide, no doubt.

    Lau.   Pray read.

    Har. (*reading with difficulty.*)

        " Lady, be warned !
There's more than at the chess-board met the eye ;
        Be warned !
Dark fraud and forgery do triumph else !
               A Friend."

Such billets flow not from the friendly pen :—
Ever device of some ignoble mind.
Still, something whispers me, all is not right.

Lau. Could I in supernatural agents trust,
That apparition had confounded me.
Its words, though in relation to our board,
And seeming innocent, were yet pronounced
With such malign intent, that I could not
But hold them as equivocal.
  Har.   No doubt:
Though evils, dimly seen, oft move us more
Than those most palpable to sense and view.
  Lau. But judge of my astonishment, e'en grief,
In noting the effect on Mordaunt's mind.
I fear there's something wrong : aghast he stood
Just like some guilty thing, struck dumb with fear.
Give me the honest counsel of a friend.
  Har. No state on earth ensures felicity :
Yet she who weds the dissipated man,
Entails upon herself sure misery :—
Better be wooed by poverty, in rags,
Than by the wealthy spendthrift, clad in gold !
  Lau. To wean him from this course, I still have hope.
  Har. A vain, an idle hope, I fear !—Trust not
Reform of him, once wedded to the bottle :
The foster-parent of a thousand crimes !
  Lau. Assurance having daily, of reform,
Methought amendment, we perceived of late ;
So could not but be flattered, while we feared.
  Har. True reformation is the work of time :
When earnest, it commences with the heart,
Which contrite, seeks the shades of solitude,
With fervent aspirations unto Heaven.
I've said enough, perhaps too much. Beware !
  Lau. Your words are not thrown waste upon the winds,
But take deep root within this anxious breast :
Yet, my soft friend ! where may we turn for hope ?
  Har. Count not on aid, save from superior source :
Thence only, aid can spring.
  Lau.   I know it well ;
So daily, in my orisons, fail not
To recommend him there. If prayer can save,
Mordaunt I trust is not yet lost !
  Har.   But mark ;
He and my brother come this way. Full long
It is, since they have held communion thus.
  Lau. Would it might lead to closest bonds of love !
How changed ! How haggard is his mien !—How pale !
  Har. How earnestly engaged !—Let us withdraw.
          [*Exeunt.*

Enter WARDLAW *and* MORDAUNT.

Mor. Much need I have, kind Wardlaw, of your ear.
Estranged of late I have been from your bosom,
Yet, in the hour of grief, I know its worth.
　Ward. My heart, dear Mordaunt, has been ever yours;
Though wrung to find you so estranged of late.
You know the price our youth fixed on each other:
Would that, e'en now, you proffered me your love,
As in those days!
　Mor. 　　　　　Speak not of former days,
Of blissful sunny days, no more to shine;
Of days, when I was innocent and pure!
Denounce me, rather, as a worthless wretch,
Unfit to hold fair commerce with the good,
Than name me e'er deserving of your love!
I am a guilty man!—low fallen! Yes,—
Low fallen, Wardlaw, to the depths of shame:
Past all redemption!
　Ward. 　　　　No man can be so!
There is a spirit of redeeming love,
Forever hovering around the soul,
That will sustain it when it cries for aid.
　Mor. Would I had sought that aid in season fit
Nor should I be this day, abandoned thus,
To madness,—to despair!
　Ward. 　　　　　　Mordaunt, my friend,
You grieve me sore. What can I do for you?
　Mor. O Wardlaw, Wardlaw! I am sick at heart!
　Ward. The true physician ne'er prescribes relief,
Until the patient's state is fully known.
　Mor. What balmy drug can sooth the wounded spirit?
What surgery bind up the broken heart,
And, most of all, the shattered reputation?
　Ward. Unworthy am I to be styled a friend,
By one who turns the key upon his thoughts,
Fearing to trust them to his sacred charge
　Mor. I am a pestilence!—You'll fly me?
　Ward. 　　　　　　　　No!
Ah, no!
　Mor. You'll pity me?
　Ward. 　　　　　Perhaps I may;
Yet, though I pity, still, my heart is true.
　Mor. Give me your hands; hide, hide these burning
　　cheeks;
Lend me your ear, for trust I not the tale,
Save in soft whispers, breathed at friendship's shrine!

[*Throws himself into* WARDLAW'S *arms, and remains for
some time whispering:* WARDLAW *appearing alternately
surprised, agitated, and horror struck.*]

Such then, the fatal truth, now hate me! fly!
Ward. Around you, rather would I throw my arms,
With Heaven's good will to save you!
Mor.   Frightful deed!
Ward. Tremendous act, most true!
Mor.   Betray me not!
Ward. A man betrays himself, who doubts his friend!
Mor. Then pity, Wardlaw, and direct my course!
Ward. The course that you should tread, is plainly
    marked.
None else exist.
Mor.   In mercy point it out!
Ward. To heaven for pardon sue,—forgiveness crave
Of much offended man—
Mor.   Who never pardons!
Though, heaven may!
Ward.   Heaven sure will!
Mor.   What shall I do ?
Ward. Make prompt disclosure of the deed
Mor.   To whom ?
Ward. To Fenton, surely!
Mor.   You do mock me!
Ward.   Nay!
Mor. I hoped you were my friend.
Ward.   I am, indeed,
And as a brother, honest counsel give!
Mor. Huge Chimboraso, I had thought you'd pile,
Height above height upon the fatal truth,
Sooner than whisper it to mortal ear!——
As well might I, to Laura trump my shame,
As trust it to the keeping of her father!
Ward. His mind, sublimed by holy, pious views,
Benignantly beholds the faults of youth,
For what his christian goodness can't prevent,
His christian charity essays to hide.
Mor. The fund replacing first, withdraw the check.
Ward. Impossible! Who can that draft control,
Save Fenton? He, the drawer, only can.
Mor. By heaven, you do astound my guilty soul!
O rash! O vile! O sottish damning deed!
Ward. With Fenton safety is, but with the bank,
The rigid course of law, alone prevails.
Mor. May ruin rather overwhelm my hopes,

Than brook the scorn of Laura Fenton!
 Ward.   She,
She'll pity and forgive!
 Mor.   Far rather die,
And glut the vulture's greedy beak, than live,
A pensioned mendicant, on woman's pity:
On her's, forsooth, whom I would call my wife!
No more! It blights my heart with mad'ning thought.
I can no longer bear to dwell on it!—No more!
No more! I am incapable to think.
 Ward. Let me think for you.
 Mor.   Never! Never!—No—
Nor will I e'er admit it to my heart.
 Ward. Then are you lost!
 Mor.   Far rather let me be:
Though never lost, while this my stay! [*drawing a dagger.*
 Ward.   You're mad!
Fly rather to the word of truth.
 Mor.   No more!
Mere priestcraft, to deceive and snare mankind!
Of late, far better faith is wisely taught:
Nor hope, nor fear, need give our souls dismay,
Neither in this world, nor in that to come!
Still, I'm entangled in the mystic toils,
In which, like some poor bird, I'm luckless trapt!
To extricate myself, I could break up
The sacred fount from which I drew my life!
Yes!—Yes, I'm mad indeed! O where on earth
Is hope for vrerch like me!—All's dark despair!
I'm lost! I'm lost! Let me escape myself;
Yes, though I plunge me in eternal night! [*Exit.*
 Ward. O miserable, hapless man indeed!
Yet means to save him, e'en against his will,
Must be devised; and that, with speedy zeal!
The worthless dross purloined, shall be replaced,
To mend, thus far, at least, the fearful breach.
This I may haply do—
Time flies apace!—No moment's to be lost!
So bear me on thy wings, sweet charity,
While in thy name, I do thy holy work! [*Exit.*

SCENE II.

[*An apartment in the house of* RIDGEFORD. RIDGEFORD
aud CELESTINA.]

 Ridg. The scheme last night, was cunningly contrived,
How little did I dream, 'twas plot of yours.

Cel. Why, at the moment that I left the ball,
Blind chance, threw in my path a maniac elf,
That won my notice by its antic gibes.
From parched and shrivelled lips, a hideous grin,
Burst horrible, nor human seemed its voice.
The thought like lightning, flashed across my mind,
To play, in sportive mood this idle jest,
So forthwith pressed this thing to my design.
It clambered up the columns, like some sprite,
And soon returned ; having performed, I learn,
The character I cast, to admiration.
   Ridg. Beyond all sanguine hope, I can attest.
If vengeance were your end, full sure 'twere yours,
I ne'er beheld a wretch so tortured !—Yet,
'Tis pity, almost, to pursue him thus !
   Cel. Could I believe that pity moved your breast,
I'd plant a dagger there and drain from it
Each drop of kindred blood ! No more, no more !
Remember, what I was—now, what I am !
   Ridg. A foot tread !—List.
   Cel.   'Tis his !
   Ridg.   Retire ! Retire !
                             [*Exit* CELESTINA.

Enter MORDAUNT *under great excitement.*

   Mor. Ridgeford ! kind Ridgeford !—I am a ruined man !
Where'ere I turn, despair and madness reign !
   Ridg. The matter ?—Has the judgment day arrived ?
   Mor. It has !—To me, it has arrived, indeed !
My bosom's turned by conscience, inside out :
I cannot bear to think on what I've done ;
Although unworthy drunkard that I was,
When this cursed hand performed the fatal deed !
O that the grave would swallow me alive,
That this racked soul, once more might be at rest !
   Ridg. Why man, your crime, since, such you'll have it
     termed,
Is far more common than the world believes—
And what is it at most ?—A mere forced loan,
That hard necessity from avarice draws,
To be restored, with due convenient speed.
   Mor. You view the subject with a partial eye :
The law, at least, presents a sterner front
Against offenders.
   Ridg.   Law I do detest !
The scourge of innocence, the reward of guilt—
Th' invention of the strong against the weak :

The tyrant's sceptre, and the poor man's yoke—
I love that perfect freedom of the will,
That guides our path, by duty, not by fear.
    Mor. I feel, good Ridgeford, that my mind is weak,
Veering between sage counsel, knowing not
What course to steer.
    Ridg.   Be wise, and all is safe.
You have nought else to do, but silence keep.
    Mor. I have but now, consulted Wardlaw—
    Ridg.   What!—
Speak that again, lest I mistake your words.
    Mor. Who counsels prompt confession of our crime.
    Ridg. O monstrous folly! Brutal madness this!
Nor have I terms to utter half my scorn!—
What fell fatuity misguides your mind?
Full sure you're mad. You need a guardian's care!
Yet, be it so—smooth Wardlaw follow, man,
And hang!– Better to fall beneath the paw
Of lean and hungry Pard, than into hands
Of canting hypocrites!—Sure Fenton's not
Trustworthy held, and Wardlaw so, far less.
Has he, though saint, think you, no amorous eyes?
Does he look on fair Laura, and not sigh
To witness your destruction!—Are you blind?
    Mor. Just Heaven!
    Ridg.   Who e'er kept faith in love affairs?
In which all acts are held in honest part,
That reach attainment of desired ends.
    Mor. I'm over-reached, too well I do perceive.
I am supplanted, and deserve to be.
I am betrayed, and that too, by a friend!
    Ridg. No tears can blot out folly such as this:
Though tears are vain when folly mourns disgrace;
The short cut road to happiness, the best;
Which long I have pursued and will pursue.
Such, wise men ever tread, fools never find:
I'll lead you to Elysium yet, if well
You follow up the counsel that I give.
    Mor. I hang upon you as my guardian saint.
    Ridg. Then set your beaver, boldly up—as thus,
Nor doff it tamely unto any man.
And though you're racked within, let gentle smiles,
Like summer zephyrs sport upon your cheek.
He's bold indeed, who tempts the heart of one,
That firmly keeps the keys of it himself.
    Mor. And them I grasp, yea, even with my life!
No longer will I prove a knave's base dupe!
So let me fly to finish my resolves!   [*Exit.*

Enter CELESTINA.

Ridg. Our secret is already out—Behold,
He has disclosed to Wardlaw !
Cel.   Say you so ?
By evil genius sure, he seems possessed !
We still, must turn his folly to account :
Methinks I see the course, though faintly traced —
If but to Wardlaw, he'd disclosure made,
Before the ball, how easy 'twere to plant
A deadly feud between them.
Ridg.   As for that,
But little import 'tis ; as time not space,
Is measured nicely, in the drunkard's mind.
How easy to impress him with belief,
That, Wardlaw is the secret, moving cause
Of all his ills—thus he sure meets the brunt
Of his displeasure, e'en his rage.
Cel.   That's well.
Yet guard 'gainst weakness that discovers all,
Before your project's brought to full account.
Ridg. Old scores exist 'twixt Wardlaw and myself,
Which we, through Mordaunt, haply may blot out.
The most that's fit, is well to ply him.   Wine,
Ay, far more potent streams, shall flow, if need.
Come this way with me.   You must not be seen
Before our project's ripe,   When that is full,
Fail not to play your part.
Cel.   Let that be mine.
Ridg. Thus may we mould him as we best may think.
We must not leave him long to other's sway.
So let's begone – No moment's to be lost.   [*Exeunt.*

SCENE III.

A private study in the house of FENTON,—FENTON
*seated, examining a number of papers.—A gentle rap at the
door.*

Fen. Who knocks ?   Come in.

Enter WARDLAW.

Ward.   I hope I find you well.
Fen. Thank heaven, my son, in health.   And you ?
Ward.   As one
Beholding, near some trembling brink, a friend,
With will alone to snatch him from his fate.
My arm's too weak,—I need another's aid,

To perfect what my anxious soul desires.

Fen. If mine may serve 'tis ever at your call.
What may I do to forward your design?

Ward. The power exists with you, alone, to move
In this most delicate and sacred work.
Too much I've tested at those liberal hands,
To need assurance of their bounty now;
Yet, strange as this may seem, I must forestall
A sacred promise from those generous lips,
That you will not withhold the boon I crave.

Fen. Speak on. Yet, pause a moment,—some one comes.

Enter CLERK.

Clerk. A forgery, 'tis thought, of vast extent,
Was yesterday committed in your name:
At least, a draft of large amount was paid.
Suspicion has arisen, since, which rests
Upon a youth, till now of fair repute,
Though for the present justice bids us pause.
Needing the prompt attention of your house,
I come to ask your presence at our bank,
In haste.

Fen. I'll soon be with you.   [*Exit* CLERK.
                                    Tarry here.
'Tis fit I should attend without delay:
This urgent call despatched, I will return,
And further counsel hold upon this point.

Ward. O leave me, leave me not, I pray!—One word,
One word before we part,—and yet, to speak
Unmans me! I could weep! Yet, ah! how vain!
Fain would I draw the veil, and hide it ever!
But 'tis impossible!—The man, whom last
Suspicion dare assail, a deed has done,
Which from the depths of shame he mourns. Behold,
A suppliant before you, in his cause
I stand, imploring pardon at your hands!
The sum purloined is re-deposited
In bank. Such breach against another's rights,
Prompt retribution only can repair.

Fen. Pity, too often, tempts the willing heart
To acts which rigid justice disapproves.

Ward. Yet, yet, my reverend friend, consider this:
Justice fails seldom, rigidly enforced,
To wound the innocent; a thunderbolt
It is, that purifies the air, yet blasts
The oak. Avert it, sir, and spare, O spare
A youth, whom you would freely die to save.

Fen. Mysterious words !—Explain.
Ward.   Pray urge me not,
Till more convenient time discloses all.
Knowing the awful rigor of the laws,
I fly to you before it is too late !
Fen. Keen, true, the sword that justice doth unsheath
Against this high offence !—How should I shrink,
Yes, shrink with horror from the painful task,
Public avenger of a crime like this !
The judge consigns the culprit to the tree,
Yet oft himself deserves a culprit's fate.
Thus should we willing pardon grant, as we
Forgiveness need ourselves, at other's hands.
Ward. Each moment, sir, is big with life or death.
O lose not one, but grant my fervent suit !
Fen. What would you have me do ?
Ward.   An order pen
That I may be receiver of this check,
Presented in your name.   The task be mine,
To manage in this delicate affair ;
And while we spare the culprit, save a friend.
Once more, I urge you, let my suit prevail !
Fen. Well, be it so.   Take then the order,—there !
You ne'er abused a confidence reposed :
Take it, my son ; and heaven may bless your work !
                [*Handing a written paper to* WARDLAW.

Enter MR. MORDAUNT.

Ward. Who would forego a moment's joy like this,
For all that earthly treasure can procure !   [*Exit.*
Mr. Mor. What means this burst of joy ?
Fen.   Ever intent
On some benignant work, how often thus !
A heart more noble never honored man.
The love of all his due, Heaven his reward !
Mr. Mor. Would that our Leonard had but made him
    friend,
In lieu of such as misdirect his paths !
O Fenton, Fenton ! what avails us wealth,
If blessed not in the children of our love !
Fen. The days of giddy youth will pass away,
And reason will at length prevail.   We once
Were thoughtless too.
Mr. Mor.   Though not with crime beset,
Like that which now pervades our favor'd land.
Our foible ne'er was hateful love of wine,
Whatever else beset our youthful course.

Wine plucks fresh roses from the manly brow,
And twines the noxious nightshade in their place ;
Drags honor down from her exalted seat,
Making her inmate of the beggar's booth !
From other vice, there's hope of safety left,
While that leads, surely, straightway unto shame,
Amidst the loathsome horrors of disease.

 Fen. A pest more fatal, ne'er afflicted man :
Still are we bound, in Heaven's good will to trust.

 Mr. Mor. Farewell to hope, when madness fills the sail.
Behold my son, my only child, the prop,
The stay, that should be of my age !--shame ! shame !
His fragrant virtues scattered to the winds :
His health, his fame, his honor, yea his love,
And all the hopes a father's heart indulged,
All cast, mere worthless counters on the die,
Or thrown like garbage unto hungry swine !

 Fen. Mordaunt, pray hold !

 Mr. Mor.   Where is he ever found ?
Ah, not where rank and fortune had designed,
But 'midst the dissipated haunts of life,
A prey to men licentious and corrupt !

 Fen. Why dwell so long upon such painful themes ?
Come, come, dismiss them I entreat.

 Mr. Mor.   Too long
Account have I with this sad heart to hold,
Thus hastily to drive it from my thoughts.
Forever mingling in life's busy round,
I seldom pleasure sought in home's soft sports,
But much neglected my domestic joys.
A heart like his, for sympathy and love,
Could not continue long a desert waste;
So when his father, I, at length inclined
To enter in and take my goodly seat,
Behold my comely tenement possessed,
And even rifled by intruders' hands !

 Fen. How oft our children's vices may we trace
From seeds, by our own hands, in early life,
With heedless folly sworn.

 Mr. Mor.   Remorse ! Remorse !
The feast, the ball-room, and the rout were ours ;
But now behold the bitter fruits we reap !
O could I but recall the days we've spent
In sports and pastimes which no worth possess,
How freely would I yield them, now ; yea, all,
For one brief moment of domestic bliss !

 Fen. Yet grieve not thus. With joy we've noted late

Amendment in him ; so in heaven we trust,
He still may prove a comfort to our age !
  Mr. Mor. That heaven may rule it so is my first prayer,
The deep ejaculation of my heart.
Come with me, Fenton ; we must comfort her
Who needs our utmost sympathy and care.   [*Exeunt.*

ACT IV.—SCENE I.

*A garden. Moonlight. A gate-way at the back of the
    scene.* RIDGEFORD *and* CELESTINA.

  Cel. Our project works beyond most sanguine hope.
As schooled by you, I waited late on Laura,
As on mere ordinary visit bent,
Though failed not, while I held her ear, to stamp
Impressions on her anxious mind, that time
Will not too readily efface.
  Ridg.   Indeed !
Well let us hear,—how went your words ?—proceed.
  Cel. The billet I devised, full well I found,—
Though all ambiguous and penned in haste,—
Had fruitful mischief borne within her breast,
That seemed much moved 'twixt love and wounded pride.
She will no doubt dismiss him.
  Ridg.   Think you so !
'Tis well,—Now as to Wardlaw. what of him ?
  Cel. Him, to the skies I lauded, pious, sage
And true. In commendation warm, she joined
With more than well-becoming zeal, methought ;
At least, for one betrothed, and,—if report
Speaks true,—destined so early to become
A bride.
  Ridg. As to the check ?—A fruitful theme,—
No doubt you touched on that.
  Cel.   While on that head—
And forgery was bluntly spoken off,—
Which Laura seemed disposed at first, to doubt :
Denouncing it as treason 'gainst his fame,
And utterly absurd and false as base ;
In confirmation of the fact, I turned
To Wardlaw, who,—for fate would have it so —
A call of ceremony also paid.
It was amusing truly, to remark
How awkwardly he strove to waive the point,
Which seemed, however, from each faltering word,
A tenfold confirmation to derive.

Ridg. Right swiftly slander flies upon the winds;
Nor surer herald need she e'er employ
Than over-prudent friends, who'd fain the truth
Suppress.
    Cel.   How goes the work with Mordaunt? Him
You do contrive to render mad, I trust;
If not with spleen, with jealous rage, at least.
    Ridg. I hold him 'twixt my finger and my thumb:
One breath from me, quick, blows him into flame.
He's now right easily imposed upon,
Is seldom found in sober mood of late,
And may with ease be drawn to any end.
    Cel. Be wary, then, and some fit pretense seize
To bring him and good Wardlaw point to point.
What then may hap, should naught fall out more grave,—
Will give at least most plenteous scope for mirth,
And prove a town-talk, for a month at least.
    Ridg. Mordaunt would call him to the field, but knows,
That, Wardlaw holds his character too slight
Were not his sanctity most ample cloak,
His cowardice to blink beneath its folds.
    Cel. But look! Who's here? The man himself,—
    Ridg.   Be still!
    Cel. Bid the mad ocean lashed to foam, be still!
My blood boils at my heart whene'er I think!
    Ridg. Withdraw,—It is not fit you meet him now.
    Cel. I see not truly, why we should not meet,—
Yet be it so!—I shall not wander far,
But hang about his path, to weigh each word
That 'scapes his lips.   [*aside and exit through the gate.*
    Ridg. So here he comes,—no common part is mine!
Would it were past!—No time to halt,—

Enter MORDAUNT.

                     My friend!
    [*Advancing, shakes* MORDAUNT *cordially by the hand,*
Have you met Wardlaw since we parted last?
    Mor. E'en so. With low'ring brow and hasty step
I crossed his path, but no word 'scaped our lips.
He would have spoken,—Hypocrite he is!
But that, I scowled upon him with contempt
And flung his half formed words back in his throat.
    Ridg. And yet, most fatal act of ill-timed faith,
You madly laid your bosom bare, and gave
Your conscience to his faithless charge.
    Mor. With heartfelt shame, I do repent what's past.
But what is done, is done.

Ridg.   More prudence learn.
Tis better late, than never to be wise.
Mor. My mind at present swings 'twixt fear and doubt,
Like heavy portal moved by infant's hands :
But should I find him play a faithless part,
'Twere better for him he'd been never born.
Ridg. May heaven forfend you find not fatal cause
To mourn the confidence so illy placed.
As for myself, I've heard, yea, seen too much,
To doubt but you've been falsely dealt withal.
Mor. Yet, let it pass,—Suspicion is awake,
Nor can I ever be hoodwinked again.
Ridg. What I would now impart, is breathed in faith :
In fact, I should be wanting were I mute,
On topic that so interests a friend.
Mor. No doubt.
Ridg.   And yet, I go mayhap too far,
By pressing painful truths, with too much zeal.
Mor. Fear not.   My trust is boundless in your love.
Nor can I hope to make you fit returns.
Ridg. One brief word then, and I fulfil my part.
It is, perhaps, the last I e'er may urge,
So store within your heart what now I speak,—
A stranger may not press the plighted hand
Nor print the amorous kiss on lip that's pledged,
Without infringement on another's rights.
Such dalliance must be criminal, and well
The chastisement due treachery deserves :
You understand me, nor need more be urged.
Mor. By all that's just, you fill me with dismay !
Ridg. In Laura, chance for safety only dwells ;
For should some other gain her hand,—you're lost !
Yea, lost to fortune, honor, e'en to fame !
When did you meet her last ?
Mor.   Within the week ;
And when we parted, she was bathed in tears.
Since then, the darkest dens of nether hell
Have been my refuge from this hateful world !
She loves me doubtless—else, why should she weep
When e'er we part,—nay, even when we meet ?
Ridg. Woman, remember, 'tis not safe to trust :
She is as subtle as the subtle snake,
Beguiling ever, ever to beguile ;
Her smiles or tears of equal import are :
The best, no better than the worst at heart.
Woman is never to be trusted long :
Meet Laura, still, and that without delay.

No moment's to be lost :--Learn how you stand.

Mor. My presence sure, would soil her spotless soul !

Ridg. You view her now, with love sick eyes.—When
    wed,

She'll lose her gloss, and seem, as true she is,

No better than the rest of all her sex.

Let not your prudence fail you at this point.

Your state is critical and loudly claims

The utmost courage you can summon forth.

Mor. My resolution's fixed as death,—Fear not.

By fair or foul, before the morning's Sun,

Loved Laura's mine !

Enter CELESTINA *hastily.*

Perdition seize me ! Celestina here !

Cel. Yes, I am here, and tremble at my glance !

Mor. Avert those eyes ! Look not upon me thus !

O slay me not !

Cel.   Fear not thou death, poor slave !

Ridg. You will undo our schemes. [*aside to* CELESTINA.

Cel.   Why dread'st thou
    death ?

Death is but refuge for a wretch like thee :

Shame's immortality, more just, thy due !

For me, thou livest, to be the standing jest,

The sport, the plaything for my bitter hate !

Far rather hold thee up, that hand of scorn

May daily smite thy cheek !—Yes, thou shalt grow

Familiar with disgrace, and drink her cup

With tenfold keener zest, than ever babe

A mother's milk imbibed !

Mor.   Rack not my soul

Already tortured with remorse and shame !

Cel. Fear not,—Thou livest,--but like a vampire, I

Upon thy throbbing heart will perch and feed,

Exulting in thy agonized throes !

Mor. Poor triumph o'er the lost !

Cel.   True, thou art lost,

And that I joy to hear !—I loved thee once,

Yea, thou dost know how well I loved thee once,—

But now, I scorn thee !

Ridg.   Celestina hold !

Cel. I will, yes, will speak out,—Fame's busy tongue

With trump and drum, hath spread abroad thy shame,

Drunkard thou art, a forger and a thief !

Ridg. You go too far. Pray calm your rage !

Cel.   Hear this

And tremble, if of human mould thy heart !
Thy infamy sits rife on every tongue :
Wardlaw hath made it current as the winds.
Fenton's privy to it,—yea, all the world,—
Thy father, e'en thy mother curse thy birth !
   Mor. O !
   Cel.   If another truth can give thy heart
One keener pang, that truth then learn from me ;
A truth, that, most will wring thy perjured soul !—
Learn, that, e'en Laura doth abandon thee ;
For I, e'en I, have disabused her love !   [*Exit.*
   Mor. Then shame receive me ! All indeed is lost !
   Ridg. Let not mere woman's broil disturb you thus.
Despair not yet.
   Mor.   Sin's wages true, is death !
Name not despair, nor hope, nor fear to me.
With earth and earth's concerns, I now have done,
And justly, death's reward of crimes like mine.
Yet come not death, till I do sow and reap
E'en the full harvest of revenge and hate !
In flood's oblivion I will henceforth lave
Inhaling naught, but bitterness and gall,
Till demon like, I usher forth, to work
The deadliest deeds of fell and black despair !   [*Exeunt.*

SCENE II.

An apartment in the house of FENTON. WARDLAW, HAR-
RIET *and* LAURA.

   Ward. A nobler heart ne'er beat in mortal breast,
Men loved to plant their honors in that field,
Counting how rich the harvest they would reap,
But fortune, which so eagerly this world
Pursues, deceitful proved and turned his foe.
E'en wit and genius, recreant to his fame,
Their false allurements spread, and thus he fell,
Debased ; a victim at their gilded shrine.
   Lau. But for one loose companion of his youth,
He had not strayed thus far, from virtue's path !
   Ward. Ridgeford's the man, whom I have ever shunned :
He is not to be trusted, friend or foe.
Yet, Mordaunt, though with high, exalted soul,
In him a kindred spirit seeks. He's gay,
And leads, with fascinating charm the round
Of giddy joy, the fatal pathway strewing
With gallantry and wit.
   Har.   Reared in the school

Of modern infidelity, behold,
He and his sister, treat with marked contempt
All laws, both moral and divine, and scoff
At what they will not comprehend.   Indeed,
I've known them rail, until my heart waxed faint !
 Ward. Who takes our life, or rifles e'en our purse,
May some atonement make offended laws :
But what has Heaven's fierce wrath not stored for him,
Who glides into the sanctuary of peace,
And plunders it of hope !
 Lau.   Depravity,
For which the world no epithet has found.
 Ward. But yesterday I met our wretched friend,
Who had just sallied from some loathsome haunt,
Where wretchedness and vice close converse hold.
His hair dishevelied and his garment soiled,
With bloated visage and distorted eyes,
He glored upon me.   He essayed to speak,
But thick, unmeaning murmurs gurgled forth,
And accents incomplete, died on his tongue.
His reason fled,—in sorrow I passed by !
 Har. O hapless, hapless man.
 Lau.   Still save him pray !
Restore him to his friends, to honor, fame !
 Ward. The strictest search I make, e'en till he's found.
O could I meet him in a sober mood,
When reason might resume her gentle sway,
I hold withal, to tranquilize his soul,
Which late of fiercest madness seems possessed.
The hour is come, when he must move abroad.
I will rejoin you soon again,—Farewell,
To meet, I trust in happier hours than these !
           [*Exit* WARDLAW.
 Har. Farewell, dear brother !   Heaven send you speed !
Take comfort, Laura, all may not be lost.
There's hope while yet we do not cease to pray.
 Lau. O could he but be rescued from that band
Of worse than robbers, that infest his path,
There might be hope indeed : but captive held
In their dread toils, a victim bound, he seems
Prepared for slaughter at the altar's horns.
 Har. Like some stanch bark, careering o'er the main,
Dashing the white spray from her sturdy prow ;
Which slow consumed, by secret fires within,
Headlong she plunges to her briny tomb,—
Ah ! I could weep to think how sad his fate !
 Lau. Is it not wonderful, that, Mordaunt, once

The pride, the glory of admiring friends,
The ornament of life, a world's bright star ;
Howe'er by keen necessity sore pressed,—
Which well we know, cannot be truly urged,
For deed so desperate,—should condescend
To snatch a pittance both from hand and heart
At all times open to his utmost wants.
   Har. It is deplorable, and loudly speaks
How frail, how weak the stoutest mortals are,
Unless sustained by more than human strength.
   Lau. 'Tis done !—Anticipated widowhood,
Has this poor heart forever swathed in weeds !
   Har. Still, still may it please kind Heaven to recall
Our wandering friend, and lead him back to peace !
But look ! His mourning father comes !—Be still.

Enter FENTON *and* MR. MORDAUNT.

   Mr. Mor. I blush to look upon you.
[*Taking* LAURA *tenderly in his arms.*
   Lau.   Dearest Sir !
Let us take courage,—All may yet be well.
Why should we cast the lamp of hope away,
E'en though it light us only to the tomb ?
   Mr. Mor. Such flattering accents fall upon my heart,
Like drops of dew, upon the mountain waste :
They fall refreshingly, yet, bring no fruit !—
I fondly hoped to've pressed a daughter's hand ;
But all my hopes are blasted by this blow !
   Lau. Still, you shall ever, Sir, be dear to me :—
A daughter I must prove, whate'er may hap.
   Fen. Misfortunes, Mordaunt, spring not from the earth,
From high origin they take their rise,
And we are bound submissively to yield.
The man beloved of Heaven, sure Heaven reproves,
As parent oft the forward child, in whom
His anxious soul delighteth much.
   Mr. Mor.   Most true !
And had I chastened my beloved son,
As Heaven in mercy now chastises me ;
I had not been this day abandoned thus,
Unto the rigor of my own reproaches !
O Fenton ! Fenton ! much I need support !
   Fen. Look up. You must obtain that from above :
Thence only cometh help, to those who faint.
   Mr. Mor. O had he died an infant in these arms,
Then had I known the luxury to weep
Over an innocent and timely grave !

Har. Alas!

Mr. Mor.　　　Short sighted mortals as we are,
Who little know, when Heaven intends us well!
I never can forget, when once, my child,—
This same dear Leonard, whom we now deplore,—
Stretched on the bed of pain and sickness, lay.
Each moment, we expected him to die.
Close at his side, his anxious mother sat,
Knowing not truly, where to turn for hope.

　Fen. Mordaunt, O Mordaunt, spare our hearts such
　　pangs!

　Mr. Mor. Raising our trembling hands and humbled
　　hearts,
We dared, with impious lips, his life to crave;
Vowing to dedicate that life to virtue!—
Our prayers were heard! Our child was spared! He
　　lived!—
Yea, lives alas!—Our curse!

　Fen.　　　　　　　　Your blessing, yet,
Perhaps. Mysterious are the ways of grace;
Past finding out by man!

　Mr. Mor.　　　　　Thou Source of Good,
Sustain the weaker vessel, lest it sink!
This awful visitation I might bear:
My sufferings are great, yet who, just power!
Who can uphold, save thee, a doating mother,
When, like a thunder-cap, this frightful truth
Shall burst on her devoted head!

　Har.　　　　　　　　Look up.
Some angel will descend to her support,—

　Lau. And we will hover round her with our love.

　Fen. But peace, my friend!—Your wife!—Collect your-
　　self.

　Mr. Mor. Why should maternal ear be ever struck
By discord such as this!—She comes! She comes!
All ignorant of what impends, as babe,
That treads the yawning gulf!

　Fen.　　　　　　　　Support her, Heaven!

Enter MRS. MORDAUNT *in haste.*

　Mrs. Mor. Where is our son?—O tell me where is Leon-
　　ard?
Mordaunt, I pray you tell me, where's our child?—
To what can such mysterious silence tend!
In ever countenance, methinks I note
Sad index of some dread catastrophe!

Why are you here, in mournful conclave met?
Why stand as monumental marble, dumb!
Why agonize my soul by dread suspense!
O speak! O speak!—if but to say,—he's dead!
Mr. Mor. This is too much!
Har.   Too much, to bear indeed!
Mrs. Mor. The fatal truth speaks out! He's dead!
    [*She faints and drops into her husband's arms.*
Mr. Mor.   My wife!
Fen. Kind friends, a couch!—My love, bring water,—
Haste!

[HARRIET *exit hastily.* MR. MORDAUNT *and* FENTON,
support MRS MORDAUNT *and take her off.*—LAURA
overcome by violent emotions, throws herself into a seat.]

Enter MORDAUNT, *disguised in dress and flushed with
drink.*

Mor. Laura!
Lau.   Ha! Mordaunt!   [*starting from her seat.*
Mor.   Trembling girl! What say!
Seem I some form of execrable shape,
That, pale you turn, and startle at my sight?—
'Till late my Laura was not wont to act
Such part!
Lau. Nor Mordaunt, 'till of late, to read
Strange signs in Laura's eyes, if they but chanced
To light upon him with accustomed glance.
Mor. 'Tis strange! Why fix your gaze upon me thus!
Lau. More strange by far, why do you question thus?
Mor. By Heaven, you mock me!
Lau.   Nay!—you frighten me!—
Why, gentle Mordaunt, why disordered so?
Why, why in this unusual costume clad!
Why do you frown and stare upon me thus!
What is the matter? Speak,—are you not well?
What has disturbed you? say, that I may calm
If possible, your cares.
Mor.   Wardlaw! Wardlaw!
Lau. Your absence brings kind Wardlaw deep concern.
Not knowing where you were, Wardlaw has gone
To seek you.
Mor.   Ha! Indeed! How courteous grown!
I'm hunted, am I?—Well, I trust he goes
With scrip and bell, to ring me through the streets
Like some lost brat!—You then have seen him? Ha!

44

Lau. 'Tis not long since we parted here.
Mor.   Indeed !
Look steadfastly upon me, girl, and say,
Ay, truly, as you hope salvation, say,
Has Wardlaw sported with my fame or not !
    Lau. Propitious Heaven protect him !
    Mor.   Speak it out !
Give forth the truth, and from those sacred lips,
Else fell perdition shall enshrine us both !
    [*Draws a dagger and seizes her violently:* LAURA
        shrieks.
I harm you not !   [*Thrusting her rudely from him.*
            Long, long 'ere this, poor thing !
I might have winged your gentle spirit hence,
But, ——   [LAURA *sinks into a seat.*

            Enter FENTON *hastily.*

    Fen.   Whence that cry !
    Lau.   My father save me ! help !
    Mor. Merely a mouse sprang from the wainscot, there,
And moved your gentle daughter.   Nothing worse.
    Fen. What do I behold !—— —— ——— !
Is this some demon of eccentric flight,
Straggling towards earth from an inferior sphere !
Or do I dream ?—Some phantom of the night,
Perhaps, sick fancy conjures up, to scare !
    Mor. No ! It is neither phantasy nor dream ;
But, Leonard Mordaunt, Leonard Mordaunt ! Ay !
In proper person, here, before you stands,
On vengeance missioned, and on death resolved !
    Lau. I can't endure such scenes ! O let me fly ! [*going !*
    Mor. Nay Laura, Nay, you shall not leave me thus !—
I am not mad ! Look on me, girl, once more !
Yes, yes, look on me, if you ever loved ;
And tell me truly, do you love me still ?
    Lau. O spare me ! Spare me !
    Fen.   True, you are not mad,
    Mor. Yet in this brain a raging fire prevails
That, will consume and in one ruin sweep,
Without the hope of heaven, or fear of hell,—
Me and my hopes !
    Fen.   Is there a Heaven ?
    Mor.   Perhaps !
There may be ;—but, a hell there is, I know !
    Fen. Speak you of hopes !—of,—
    Mor.   Desperate revenge !

Revenge which I do reap, if heaven be true !
Fen. Although no sway you own of earthly power.
Dread still, hereafter,—
    Mor.   Wiser far than we
Have said there is not, and the thought I hail!
    Fen. Abandoned atheist !
    Mor.   Worse ! Hypocrite !—
But hold I have no time to banter thus,
And with a dotard, hold such idle prate,
I come to claim my Laura.—Yes,—my wife !
You can't withhold her hand. Come to me ! Come !
Your lawful plighted husband claims your troth.
    Fen. If you regard your health, retire !—I'm old,
Yet will protect my daughter with my life.
    Mor. By Heaven, she's mine, and I will lead her forth,
If there be truth. The altar and the priest
Await. The bridegroom and the bride are we.
This winding sheet my wedding robe,—Start not,—
As winding sheets there are for more than me !—
The feast will cool, so come with me ! Away !
    [*He makes violently towards* LAURA, *who flies into her
        father's arms.*
    Fen. Tamper not, madman, with my feelings thus !
Begone,—else I no longer stay my hand,—

        Enter Mr. MORDAUNT *hastily.*

    Mr. Mor. In mercy's name ! what fiend of mischief here !
    Mor. My father !   [*Throwing down his dagger.*
    Mr. Mor.   Leonard ! my lamented child !
        [*Advancing towards* MORDAUNT.
    Mor. Stand back ! Stand back !—I do contaminate
What e'er I touch. A leperous mass am I
That would pollute a world.
    Mrs. Mor. (*Without.*) Give way ! Give way !
The sacred name of child sounds on my ear,

    Enter Mrs. MORDAUNT *and* HARRIET *hastily.*

O where, O where's my son ?
    Mor.   My mother ! Ha !
    Mrs. Mor. Ah yes, with anxious glowing heart,
On wings of love, thy mother seeks thy arms !
        [*Embracing him eagerly.*
    Mor. Avaunt !—I am not thus to be ensnared !
Though son of thine, no slave am I !—Stand off
        [*Thrusting her rudely from him.*
    Mr. Mor. Rash youth ! What have you done !

Fen.   Thy mother thus !
Mor. If thou dost love me, mother !—fly me !
Mrs. Mor.   Never !
O Leonard, kill, but do not cast me off :
Whate'er may hap, I am thy mother still !
Brush, brush the scowl from that once placid brow,
Where the soft smiles of innocence prevailed,
And calmly look, once more upon thy mother !
Mor. Never again !—A being am I, lost !—
No father, mother, friend, or love is mine !
Forever stricken from the rolls of fame,
I hold no future fellowship with man ;
But wandering, outcast, linked with hate and woe
Dread transit make across this world of shame !
                        [*Exit, dashing out furiously.*
Mrs. Mor. O Leonard ! One,—one last farewell !
                        [*Faints and falls into her husband's arms.*
Mr. Mor.   He's fled !
All, all I fear is lost !
Fen.   Reason dethroned
Intemperance usurps her sovereign sway !
                        [*A pistol is fired without.*
                  (*A pause.*)

[*Great noise and confusion without. Repeated cries of
    murder from* RIDGEFORD *without.*]

Mr. Mor. O frightful spectacle !
Lau.   Tremendous sight !
Mr. Mor. The storm has burst !
Fen.   And ruins follows swift !
[*Enter* WARDLAW *wounded. He falls into his sister's
    arms.*
Har. Horatio !
Ward.   Sister !—My beloved girl !
He knew not what he did,—Forgive ! Forgive ! [*dies.*
  Har. He's dead !—Horatio ! [*Faints,—*LAURA *supports
    her.*
Fen.   He is dead, indeed !

[MORDAUNT *rushes in, a pistol in his hand. He makes
    furiously towards the body of* WARDLAW,—*While* FEN-
    TON *interposes. Enter* RIDGEFORD *slowly, while* MOR-
    DAUNT *bestrides the dead body of* WARDLAW. *The scene
    closes.*]

ACT V.—SCENE I.

An apartment in the house of RIDGEFORD. RIDGEFORD
and CELESTINA.

Cel. Proceed, I pray proceed!
Ridg.   Mordaunt had just
Some fierce encounter had with those within,
When rushing from the house, whom should he meet,
Aye, even at the threshold of the door
Of Fenton,—glowing with revenge ; whom meet
I say, but Wardlaw ?—Self-devoted man !—
Suspense a momentary silence breathed,
While fury gleamed portentous from each eye.
Mordaunt at length was moving off, when strange,
With sudden leap, th' infuriate Wardlaw sprang
On his retreating foe, and in his throat
Struck fast his pangs.
Cel.   Spake Mordaunt naught ?
Ridg.   He strove
With fierce convulsive throes to cast him off.
I tried myself to extricate his grasp
In vain.   Exhausted soon, faint Mordaunt grew—
And Wardlaw, doubling all his efforts, seemed
With fiend-like rage, full bent to strangle him ;
When Mordaunt, quick,—extremity for life,—
Forth from his belt a pistol luckless drew—
Which by sheer accident he'd there concealed,—
And lodged the contents in poor Wardlaw's breast !
Cel. Who had supposed it could have come to this !
Ridg. Never did man strive longer to avoid
The fatal act. 'Twas dark.   Murder the cry
Now loudly raised by me, drew forth the mob.
Wardlaw fled.   Dagger drawn, Mordaunt close pressed,
And at the door, home plunged it in his back !
Cel. So hapless Wardlaw then, is slain !
Ridg.   Too true,
Though merited his fate : nor can I say
It grieves me much.—But let me forth proceed.
Mordaunt, a fury, bent on death, rushed on
With reeking dagger in his hand.—His cry
Was often heard " I did the deed !" and seemed
To triumph in the bloody act !
Cel.   Mad fool !
Who save himself had thus proclaimed his guilt ?
Ridg. He's safe however from the grasp of law
If henceforth prudently he keeps his peace.

A word from me explains the fatal fray,
Placing him clearly on the vantage ground.
   Cel. Best see him promptly and advise the course
He should in law pursue.
   Ridg.   That leave to me.
Mordaunt made no attempt to fly. The crowd
Rushed in. The most appalling scene ensued.
Over the body, pale, his sister bent,
While Laura near her stood in mute dismay.
Apart mused Fenton, self-collected, calm.
   Cel. Just like the man! Heartless and cold as stone!
   Ridg. His mother,—but I will not speak of her!—
My heart sunk in me at the mournful sight.—
In the remotest corner of the room
Stood Mordaunt's father, statue-like and dumb!
He breathed not, spake not, while a vacant stare
Glared frightfully from his distended eyes.
He seemed unconscious of the passing scene.
Plunged wholly in unutterable grief.
   Cel. But Mordaunt—
   Ridg.   Was to prison hurried off.
   Cel. Had I foreseen this night, such scare had been.
Bad deeds like thistles, bear befitting fruit:
And ever as it should be,—ill for ill.

                 [*Noise without.*]

   Ridg. What noise! It seems like hasty feet this way!
Where hide! Where fly!
   Cel.   And wherefore would you fly?
   Ridg. Perhaps pursued—
   Cel.   Pursued!—Pursued by whom?
You're pale as death. Collect your thoughts.
The cloak of smiles, the drapery of knaves
Put on, which honesty may surely wear
When need.

                 [*Noise without.*]

   Ridg. While thus you prattle I am lost!   [*Exit.*
   Cel. Then fly—I'll plant me in the breach and front
The storm. Come then what may, I stand prepared.

      [*Enter Officer of Justice with attendants.*]

   Officer. Pardon, pray madam, this abrupt intrusion!
Your brother—Is he here?
   Cel.   Your right to know?
   Officer. No time for parley, madam—Haste,—proceed.
                 [*To attendants*

Make close pursuit and bring him forth. We know
He's here. He must be found.   [*Exeunt attendants*
     Cel.   What dark misdeed,
That thus he should be hunted like a thief ?
He had no hand in this fell act I vow !
     Officer. It ill becomes us to pretend he had :
Yet, an eye-witness to this sad affray
Attests, that Mordaunt had no sooner fired,
Than Ridgeford struck, with his own hand, the blow
By which unhappy Wardlaw met his fate !
     Cel. 'Tis false I do pronounce—I know 'tis false !
May blisters fester such deceitful lips !
My brother shall confront and put to shame
So vile a wretch !
     Officer.   If innocent, I trust
He may !
     Cel.   If innocent ! You doubt it then !
     Officer. They've apprehended him ! We must begone !
                                                  [*Exit.*
     Cel. Who could have dreamt, in soundest sleep, of this !—
Detection ! ah ! 'tis there the foiler lurks
That oft defeats the boldest schemes of hate !—
Entrapped ? Entrapped ! Escape through wit or chance !
Fool ! fool !—But since he is involved, by—— !!
He shall not fall alone ! If the storm bursts,
Why, burst it shall on other heads than ours !

             [*Enter Ridgeford in custody of Officer.*]

     Ridg. Since innocence and guilt thus share alike,
As well be guilty if it suits one's ends !
     Cel. Fear not, good brother, your's the manly part—
Go, Heaven protects the innocent and brave.
     Ridg. Farewell ! I pray you join me soon !
     Cel.   I will.
                    [*Exeunt Officer and Ridgeford.*
It grieves me sore—yet since it comes to this,
Why let it fall !—I would not have undone
The work, although it better might have been.
More easy 'tis by far to set the wheels
Of mischief on, than regulate their speed.
The cup that I have taken to my lip
Is gall, though still I'll drain it to the dregs !   [*Going.*

             [*Enter* FREEMAN *in haste.*]

     Free. A moment lady, one brief word in haste.
     Cel. What would you ? Speak !

Free.   It interests you much
Report has reached you of this sad out-break ?
You've had no doubt particulars.
    Cel.   I have.
    Free. This moment come I from the prison, where
Poor Mordaunt lies.   Counting on you his friend,
He bade me haste to crave your presence there,
With presence of your brother.
    Cel.   Strange to tell,
They will be inmates there together soon.
They strive to link my brother with the crime,
And even now have hurried him to prison.
    Free. He seems a wretch undone.   All that he speaks
Is wild and incoherent.   Now he calls
For wine, and then in suppliant tone, entreats
For brandy, to assuage his raging thirst.
Deep draughts of water slake him not.   His lips
Are parched by raging fire within, which seems
In lurid shapes to flit across his mind.
So strangely does his fancy conjure forms,
He sometimes gambols with the vacant air,
But grasping nought, convulsively he breaks
In laughter forth of horrid note.
    Cel.   Most strange !
    Free. Sometimes he plucks one by the sleeve, to seize
Rich jewels one might count of costly worth—
And now behold him crouch upon the floor,
And like an infant, sport with empty straws.
    Cel. This must be madness of no common type.
    Free. He seemed at one time in abstraction lost,
Then starting suddenly, he cried aloud
I'm innocent ! and implicated straight
His friend.
    Cel.   My brother say you?
    Free.   Even so.
    Cel.   He then appears to know you .
    Free.   Yes, full well.
He called me by my name, and spoke me kind.
He drew me near him, then entreated me
If spark of pity ever warmed my breast,
To send him poison by some secret hand.
    Cel. Art sure !
    Free.   He said, some chymic distillation
That would afford him rest : he added sleep,
The sleep of death !
    Cel.   And would he, think you, drink ?
    Free. Too sure I fear he would !

Cel.   You are his friend?
Free. I am—at least a friendly part intend.
Cel. Then would you not convey it him?—say, speak!
Free. You wrong me greatly to suspect me thus!
Cel. Hold you 'tis crime at such a time as this?
Free. I'd shudder did my mind conceive the thought.
Cel. You will perhaps a potion bear my brother?
                                        [FREEMAN *starts.*
He'd hail you as some angel, come to draw
His bolts and prison bars.
    Free.   Terrific thought!
Cel. Your pigmy monster on a fig; hideous
Yet too contemptibly minute for note.
A youth of firmness as I count you are,
You will not falter at a point like this.
    Free. You do me wrong, nor do I blush to own
Misgivings here—fears that hereafter—
    Cel.   Cease.
I would not hear you descant on such themes,
Fit award souls congenial with your own.
Go make confession to some hoary priest,
Go pay for absolution at his hands,
And come forth then, mayhap fair youth, as snow.
I find you boast not e'en a woman's nerve.
    Free. Lady, I cry you mercy.
    Cel.   Childish dreams!
The mad creation of some sickly brain!
Sooner I'd bear the burthens of a beast,
And drudge the live-long day for scanty food,
Than move at large, base slave of such conceits.
Future awards await no crimes done here,
And cowards only tremble at hereafter.
'Tis but to die, trust me, and there's an end
Of us and our concerns; at least our cares—
Such my philosophy.
    Free.   Not mine! Not mine!
Cel. Still you may not decline the humble task,
To bear in secret to my brother, such
As I'd commit into your honest charge—
It shall not go without reward—
    Free.   Reward!
Change peaceful conscience for a world's base pelf!
The hope of heaven for certainty of woe!
I cannot, will not, part or lot in this!
    Cel. Scruples like these become not e'en a girl.
I will see Mordaunt—To the prison then.   [*Exeunt.*

SCENE II.

An apartment in the house of FENTON. *The body of*
WARDLAW *lies on a bier covered with a pall. Two
lamps burning, one at the head, the other at the foot of
the corpse.* HARRIET *in deep meditation, seated by the
side of the bier. She remains for some time, then slowly
rises, and leans affectionately over the body.*

Har. Thou sainted spirit of departed goodness!
If it be given to revisit earth,
And to take part in what concerns us here,
O do thou hover over and sustain
Thy fainting sister!—
Brother beloved! art thou forever gone!
Is then the link that joined our hearts dissolved
And severed quite! Ah, yes! we part, we part
To meet no more this side the grave! 'Tis done!

Enter FENTON.

Fen. Sweet child! sure full indulgence you have had—
'Tis time to rouse from lethargy like this
To soar upon the wings of pious hope.
The live-long night here have you sat and mourned
This dear yet senseless clay:—Just tribute paid
The dead—but duties are there which you owe
The living.—Rise—perform them as becomes
The Christian!
Har.   Morning dawns. Let me go wake
Our loved Horatio.—No. He wakes no more!
Ah! never, never more, until the great,
The Resurrection morn!
Fen.   But then!
Har.   Ah then!
Transcendent and triumphant thought! Ah, then!
My darling I shall clasp again, I trust,
A pure immortal spirit, bright arrayed
In robes ætherial of celestial love,
Forever dwelling with the just made pure!

Enter LAURA.

Lau. Harriet, my sister dear! How fare you now?
Har. I feel me much refreshed—quite brave!
Lau.   Come then,
Retire with us. You must require repose.
Har. Not yet, not yet!—They come to bear away
The dear remains.

[Enter four Mutes in mourning suit, who take their stations around the bier.]

I look on them once more !

[She leans over the body, tenderly embracing it.

The Christian's sleep, at peace with all the world !
Even at peace with him who shed his blood !
Can ever I forget his dying words ?
For pardon sueing on his slayer's head.—
I freely pardon you, with all my soul !
Yes, Mordaunt, freely I do pardon grant
For his dear sake who craved it at my lips !

Lau. O grant that Heaven may pardon too !
Fen.   Amen !

[A distant bell tolls.

Har. Thou iron tongued herald,—I obey !
So now, farewell, sweet brother !—One kiss more.
And then we part forever and forever '

[Bell tolls—Exeunt all slowly.

SCENE III.

[The interior of a prison. MORDAUNT *starts suddenly from a couch on which he reclined.]*

Mor. The walls are wrapped in flames !   All is on fire !
Tear off my vestments ! Save me, O save me !
In lurid flakes the tempest rages on,
As though the last dread day were e'en at hand
And this great globe itself were summoned forth
To give its last account ! What spectre shades,
Evolving forms that revel in the flames
Hooting and shouting as they sweep along !
Avaunt, Avaunt ! Right well I know that form.
The squalled imp assailed my peace before,
And now returns to blab my guilt again !

[He crouches to the floor in great terror and covers himself with the bed clothes.]

A ceaseless torrent on my aching head
That chills the inmost fibres of my brain.
An arctic iceberg lashed by torrid storms !
Will genial warmth e're thaw again these veins
Which now seem locked in everlasting frost !

[He is seized with a violent shuddering, which after a while gradually subsides.]

Thank Heaven, the chill has passed and I am free —
Yes, once more free from this infernal charm—

And yet, most strange, e'en while the spell was on
He quaffed a bumper to me as I led
My Laura to the altar.—Soft she came,
E'en as some angel from the realms of light,
And hovered gently over me.—But look !
What light phantastic troops rise from the floor ?
Each like Goliah, armed with spear and shield.

[*He stoops and seems engaged with minute objects on the floor.*]

(*Enter* CELESTINA.)

Come hither hell-chick, perch upon my thumb.
The nimble footed train !—all fled—all fled !
   Cel. The potion that I drank has nerved my arm.
I needed such to fit me for the task
And bear me to the issue of my work.
   Mor. They all are mine.   Not one escapes.   Not one
But meet to deck an eastern monarch's bride.

(*Starts from the floor.*)

Ha Celestina !   Dawns the morn at last ?
The banns you have forbid, they say.—O rare !
Yes, passing strange, that you should interpose.
Full well you know we never plighted vows—
And if we had, 'twere wise we forfeit them.
Where is your brother ?
   Cel.   Joins us here anon.
   Mor. We hold it vastly rude that he comes not
To greet us on our wedding day.   So 'tis :
Friends oft forsake us when we need them most.
   Cel. How close allied are wit and madness oft—
Right shrewdly said.
   Mor.   Accept you one of these ?
Come, take one pray, and wear it for my sake ;
For sake of him who one day loved you well—
And would have loved you to this hour.—But hist !
   Cel. That is a word well nigh disarms my hate
Luring the ruffian purpose from my soul !   [*aside.*
   Mor. A death-bell toll !—Heard you the knell ?   Flash,
     flash !
   Cel. O frightful sight !
   Mor.   Yet tremble not, although
In sullied shroud, snatched from some timeless grave,
Eternal wrath there high has reared a throne,
Sitting in judgment on our guilty souls !
This husky dryness !   It consumes my life !

The waves of boundless ocean cannot quench
Such raging thirst !

[*Becomes suffocated and strives to relieve himself by pluck-
ing, it might seem, quantities of hair out of his mouth.*

No Leech's skill is there,
Nor potent charm, nor cunning art to pluck
This all enduring torment from my throat !
Out, out upon you !—O for a moment's rest !
 Cel. My heart misgives. Doth guilt no stouter prop
Afford her fainting votaries !—Yet hold !
Why tremble thus when but a madman raves !
Down then, base fear, down into hell thy den ! [*aside.*
 Mor. Say to your brother—I will not betray,
Although that squalled monster raves and tempts
And mocks and grins, and shakes his grisly main !
Why lags your brother thus ?—What can he fear !

 (*Enter* RIDGEFORD *from the interior of the cell.*)

O rapturous moment of reviving bliss !
I joy to meet you, Wardlaw. Welcome thrice !
Where is the fatal stab so late received ?
'Tis sad you perished by a ruffian's hand ;
Though praised be Fate, 'tis as I find a dream !

[*Shaking Ridgeford, the while heartily by the hand, then
suddenly turns aside, lost in abstraction.*]

 Cel. You come by times. I'd well nigh sank with fear.
       [*Aside to Ridgeford.*
 Ridg. Why Mordaunt, do you not recall your friend ?
 Mor. My friend ?—Say friend ? When had I pray a
  friend ?
Go cleanse them off—you've stains upon your hands—
I've seen enough of blood and crave no more.
 Cel. Who could have looked for this ? He's quite de-
  ranged.
 Ridg. As ever maniac was.
' *Cel.*   I hold it strange !
Tis come upon him like a summer's cloud.
 Ridg. " Mania a potu," as physicians say—
Now, lack of wine, as late, excess of it
The cause.—The drunkard's certain doom. He comes.
 Mor. I will disclose the whole.—Go to, I say.
A tale I could unfold would chill the soul !--
'Twas Ridgeford planned the forgery of the check.
He 'twas who placed the pistol in my hand.
'Twas he who plunged the dagger in his back !—

Let him and Wardlaw settle that account.
  Cel. Now mark you that?
  Ridg.   I weigh full well each word.
Since so to us, the like he prates to others.
  Mor. The money honest Ridgeford holds in hand,
Fair Sinclair, shall be yours.   [*To Celestina.*
  Cel.   What can he mean?
  Mor. I leave it you by will.
  Cel.   Explain you that!
  Ridg. In measure sooth with other mad conceits.
This babble, sane or frantic will ne'er do.
We must contrive to stay this nimble tongue,
Else soon it brings us ill!
  Cel.   Look here on this!—
Such have I brought, lest chance there might be need.

[*Discovering to Ridgeford a phial concealed in her man-
tle.*]

  Ridg. What is't?
  Cel.   Let him but taste,—you're safe.
  Ridg.   Indeed!
Then give it me!—We seal those lips full soon.
  Mor. (*sings.*) " Had I a heart for falsehood framed,
        " I ne'er could injure thee!"
  Cel. So now, my task is done!—I do rejoice
I have so far moved on!—I breathe once more!   [*aside.*
Mordaunt, we part!
  Mor.   Nay, leave us not thus soon.
  Cel. Poor wretch, poor wretch! forever we do part!
                 [*partly aside.*
  Mor. Too soon boon friends do part.—Bright chanticleer
Has not yet piped his matin note, but sits,
Good honest dotard, midst his wily mates,
Nor counts the fleeting hours made but for slaves—
Come—one glass more before you leave us. Fill.
  Cel. Yes—I have settled my accounts with thee—
So now farewell!—farewell!—We meet no more,
Though in that thought alone, is summed up all
My woe!   [*aside, and exit.*
  Ridg. Here, see!   (*exhibiting to Mordaunt the phial.*)
  Mor.   Ha! Let me clutch thee!—Come,

[*Seizing the phial with avidity.*]

Come to my lips, loved cordial of delight,
Come, cheer once more this sinking soul of mine! [*drinks.*
Not all the streams that gush from rock or mound,

That flow from fountain or that glide through mead,
Can half refreshment give to my parched soul,
As but one drop from the cercean cup !
Come once again !   [*Drinks.*
  Ridg.   Man's refuge and sure stay.
" Drink deep or taste not," sang th' immortal bard.
  Mor. Well said. Ah ! how reviving ! Fill again. [*drinks.*
In sage Anacreontic verse respond,
" With glowing wreaths of roses crowned,
" We pass the cheerful goblet round."
  Ridg. I shared with you the last I had.
  Mor.   Thanks, thanks !
But one drop more—and then I bide content.
  Ridg. You'll quite contented bide with that you have.
                                        [*aside.*

  Mor. Fly not the bowl !
  Ridg.   I will return anon.
  Mor. When you return, remember—wine !
  Ridg.   Ay.--Wine !

[*Exit* RIDGEFORD, *slowly, through the back of the cell.*
  MORDAUNT *remains for some time in a state of abstrac-*
  tion, then eagerly applies the empty phial to his lips.]

  Mor. Not one drop flows ! My soul for one drop more
To quench this raging fire within my breast !
Yet, why comes this ! An ugly pain sits here,
Far more voracious and more dread than hell !
The furies do beset me ! Wardlaw hold—
Reek not your vengeance on my guilty head--
Pluck me, O pluck me from the fatal pit !—
And gentle Laura ! She forsakes me too !
In flames I perish !--None to save me !—Lost !

[*Falls senseless to the floor.*]

Enter FENTON and MR. MORDAUNT *hastily.*

  Mr. Mor. Most fatal moment, what do I behold !
The wrath of Heaven, sure fallen on our house !

[*Discovering the empty phial.*]

Rash boy, rash boy ! what have you here not done ?
O how, how thus afflict a father's heart !
  Fen. Thy father speaks.
  Mor.   My father, said you not ?—
This horrid tingling in mine ear distracts—
Did you not say my father ?—Poor old man !

Where is he? Well I know he loved me dear.

Fen. This wrings my soul!

Mor.   He'll drown in tears, in tears
When he knows all. Still, bid him come to me.
I would not have him know the worst.—Nor she—
Had I not once a doting mother? Say—
A dying son would speak with them once more,
And secret of dread import would impart.

Mr. Mor. I'm here—your loving father, Leonard, here!
Do you not know me? Speak!

Mor.   Who are you pray?
I say you cannot be my father. No,
Ah no! Think you I'm cheated thus, (*laughing wildly.*)
    His heart
Was glowing. Cold as stone is thine. I knew
My father once.—To me he e'er was kind,
Yes, just and liberal as the genial sun;
But I have proved a most ungrateful child!
I broke his heart they say; mine now is wrung.

Mr. Mor. O speak not thus! Thy father pardons all
But for one look of recognition now!

Mor. Sad retrospect!

Mr. Mor.   Think no more of the past!
Would I had died 'ere I had seen this day!

Mor. Cursed be the day when first I saw the light!
Cursed be the light that brings me to this hour!

Fen. A soul responsible, on time's dread brink,
Unconscious of the plunge too soon it makes!

Mor. Most cruel stab was that! (*writhing in agony.*)

Mr. Mor.   My boy! Dear boy!

[*Raising him tenderly in his arms.*]

Mor. How soft!—Here could I sink to sleep methinks;
A wearied babe upon a mother's breast!
But off! (*struggling convulsively,*) I cannot stand another
    thrust
Like this!—Another such, and all is over!
What would you more than this poor mortal part!
Ye will not drag both soul and body too,
Down to the depths of everlasting night!
O how they gnaw and tear, and wrench my heart!
The fiends of hell beset on every side
And pour down hot damnation on my head!
Save me! O save me! Help!   [*dies.*

Mr. Mor.   The spirit's fled!

[*Falling upon the body of his son.*]

(*A pause.*)

Fen. But whither fled—who shall presume to speak !
Intemperance, thou monster crime !   Parent
Of every sin when bold and sturdy grown.
Fiends laughed, while angels wept when thou wert born :
For never since the fall hath deadlier curse
Beset the race of guilty man !

[*A piercing shriek from without*—MRS. MORDAUNT, HAR-
    RIET *and* LAURA, *rush in.*   MRS. MORDAUNT *casts her-
    self upon the bodies of her husband and son.*   FENTON
    supports HARRIET *and* LAURA.]

THE POEM CLOSES.